# FICTION

**A HAZARD OF THE JOB**
Coy Hall . . . . . . . . . . . . . . . . . . . . . . . . . . . . . . . . . . . . . . . . . . . . . . . . . . . . 2

**SIR OXNARD**
Jeffrey Hunt . . . . . . . . . . . . . . . . . . . . . . . . . . . . . . . . . . . . . . . . . . . . . . . . 13

**SCREEN SHOT**
Teel James Glenn . . . . . . . . . . . . . . . . . . . . . . . . . . . . . . . . . . . . . . . . . . . 20

**SETTING THE PICK**
April Kelly . . . . . . . . . . . . . . . . . . . . . . . . . . . . . . . . . . . . . . . . . . . . . . . . . 29

**TOMBSTONE DODGE**
Vincent H. O'Neil . . . . . . . . . . . . . . . . . . . . . . . . . . . . . . . . . . . . . . . . . . . 42

**STAR WITNESS**
Joe Giordano . . . . . . . . . . . . . . . . . . . . . . . . . . . . . . . . . . . . . . . . . . . . . . 47

**WIPEOUT**
Adam Meyer . . . . . . . . . . . . . . . . . . . . . . . . . . . . . . . . . . . . . . . . . . . . . . . 58

**THE CORPSE AT THE FOOT OF MY BED**
Gordon Linzner . . . . . . . . . . . . . . . . . . . . . . . . . . . . . . . . . . . . . . . . . . . . 72

**POISONED RELATIONSHIP**
A You-Solve-It By Laird Long . . . . . . . . . . . . . . . . . . . . . . . . . . . . . . . . 80

# INQUIRIES & ADVERTISING

**Address:** Suite 22, 509 Commissioners Road West, London, Ontario, N6J 1Y5
**Advertising:** Email info@mysteryweekly.com
**Editor:** Kerry Carter  **Publisher:** Chuck Carter  **Cover Artist:** Robin Grenville-Evans
**Submissions**: https://mysteryweekly.com/submit.asp
**Mystery Weekly Magazine** is published monthly by AM Marketing Strategies. The stories in this magazine are all fictitious, and any resemblance between the characters in them and actual persons is completely coincidental. Reproduction or use, in any manner of editorial or pictorial content without express written permission is prohibited. Copyright on stories remain with the artist or author. No portion of this magazine or its cover may be reproduced without the artist's or author's permission.

MYSTERY WEEKLY MAGAZINE

# A HAZARD OF THE JOB

## Coy Hall

No blame, no scorn in a label like feebleminded—just an inferior creature protected from a world that meant harm. Locked away for their safety and your safety. Saying feebleminded gave one the feeling of paternalism. Indeed, it was a word you could put at the top of stationary and feel good about. Only the older doctors used lunatic for the nomenclature, and when one of the doctors said *that* word tension could flood a room. Three decades had passed since lunatic had been part of the hospital's name and two decades had passed since asylum had been part of the name. Both terms were features of a regrettable past, the board said. It was a much younger board now, having jettisoned a few elder statesmen after the war. The same board, in 1922, rebranded the hospital as The State Hospital of the Feebleminded and Infirm—bland, innocuous, paternal. The name deflected attention.

The hospital stood on an idyllic hilltop ten miles from the nearest city. A narrow road winded upward from the valley at a steep grate. Between the road and hospital grounds stood an iron gate topped with baroque fleurs-de-lis, trimmings to admire if one cared to linger and look. Beyond the gate, a complex of six buildings crowded by pines and cedars sprawled like a village. The surrounding woods concealed walking paths and hillside graves. In the autumn, which held on to color that year in Virginia, the gothic centerpiece, the original 1867 building with its sandstone façade and slender windows, gratuitous turrets, and clock tower, resembled an old university in New England. Upon approach, however, despite the leaves and crisp air, the illusion would fade. Iron bars formed grilles on the windows.

Olsen, like most of the attendants, lived in a dormitory at the western edge of the complex, a brick structure crammed between a vegetable garden on one side and the airy tuberculosis ward on the other. In the garden, frost glazed a mix of pumpkins and dead stalks and upturned roots. Olsen's shift had begun at 7:00 am. Presently, with a cigarette locked between his fingers, he stepped out into the cold October morning. The breeze held a touch of winter. He took a drag on the cigarette to gird himself, and then he checked his watch. He was late. His head ached from too little coffee. Taciturn and sluggish, he started across the gravel on a footpath that led to the TB ward.

Olsen ascended the building's wide stairway, passed faux columns, and entered through double doors. The air on the first floor was warm. A nurse working reception, surrounded by a bustle of activity, greeted him with a sour expression. A cathedral radio on the desktop droned headlines. The broadcaster's rapid cadence fit the tense atmosphere. Olsen winked at the nurse, and then mashed out his cigarette in a receptacle by the door. The woman was unimpressed.

Another attendant, Mallory, the man who had gotten Olsen hired originally, rushed over. He held an armful of blankets and his face was ruddy from cold and excitement. He handed the bundle to Olsen.

Animated, Mallory said, "We found her up there with the old man again this morning."

Olsen's face reddened. He'd been on duty the night prior. "You're kidding. I know I locked that door." He sounded more certain than he felt.

Mallory shrugged. "It was locked. That's ten times in two weeks. She was sleeping when I found her. She didn't even try to leave. He was staring at the window like he does."

Of late, it was an exchange the two men seemed to renew each morning. The odd case could build into trouble for both of them, Olsen knew. He worried for his job. Besides that, being outsmarted continually by the feebleminded looked bad.

"How in the hell is she doing it?" Olsen asked. "Scaling the front wall?" *The old man's an invalid*, he thought. *He couldn't let her inside*. "You don't think they're ... uh—"

Mallory chuckled. "You know what I think." He was a short man, rotund, and his clean-shaven face held a greasy sheen. He cut his own hair and it showed. Generally, he meant well, and when he didn't mean well, he was good for laughs. "Anyway, Doc Kobel ain't pleased," he continued. "He's up there now, ranting about it to Dr. Mundy."

"Mundy didn't say anything about me, did he?" Olsen wanted his cigarette again. He checked the nurse at reception and then glanced at the smoldering remains. Soft music played on the radio.

Mallory grinned, showing a chipped tooth. "Seems like he was aware of the time. It's nearly half past, buddy. Get those blankets upstairs and try not to make eye contact with Mundy. Or Kobel. They're pissed."

Olsen cursed himself.

It was afternoon when Olsen saw her again. She was in the main courtyard, strolling along the contour of the fence. She'd escaped Kobel and Mundy's wrath, as she always managed to do. The sky was gray, the sun veiled. A breeze moved the trees, and fallen leaves covered the lawn. The air was fragrant. Bundled in a coat, she walked with her head bowed, kicking through the leaves in a way that was meditative rather than playful. A few layers of thought buried her, it seemed.

"I'm taking a break," Olsen said to anyone within earshot.

When no one protested, he started down the stairwell. At the front door he lit a Chesterfield and gazed around. The courtyard was busy with the non-violent patients milling about and getting their daily exercise, attendants and nurses crisscrossing between wards, and two large trucks idling in front of the main building. He found her on a bench near a sassafras tree, sitting alone, her hands clasped and head down, a withered pose. Nursing the cigarette, he started towards her.

Her name was Avery Sarsfield and, to Olsen, she was an enigma. She had been a patient at the hospital for five months. There was nothing obviously wrong with her, she was not insane and she was not a criminal, but she'd been judged feebleminded by a foster guardian and deposited here. The hospital worked that way. As part of a new eugenics initiative in Virginia, the state was eager to round up white trash for sterilization, to eliminate the breeding of inferiors. If that meant having doctors stamp uneducated women as feebleminded, then that is what the state demanded. The hospital complied. Dr. Kobel had, whether he believed it truly or not, approved the designation, assigning Avery Sarsfield the mental rank of moron, slightly above the IQ of idiots in the hierarchy of feeblemindedness. The classification put her on the fast track to sterilization, and she'd undergone the procedure after a month of residence. She would, like an increasing number of men and women in her class, never be allowed to reproduce. The state felt that was important with the poorer classes. As Oliver Wendell Holmes said in the Supreme Court, "Three generations of imbeciles is enough." So be it.

That much was known. Why Avery Sarsfield insisted on risking her health by frequenting the tuberculosis ward was less clear. She was not sick. Olsen and Mallory had their theories, as did Drs. Kobel and Mundy, but only Avery knew the truth.

She kept her eyes on the ground as Olsen approached. Generally, she treated attendants like they were fiends, physically recoiling in their presence. He brushed leaves from the bench, then took a seat at her side. He offered her a fresh cigarette from the pack.

Subtly, she declined. She began wringing her hands, uncomfortable.

Olsen exhaled a cloud of smoke. He crossed his legs and leaned back against the slats. "What's your story?" he asked.

Without moving, she looked at him from the side of her eye. She was very young, no more than eighteen, with mousy hair cut above her shoulders. It had been a trendy bob a year prior, no doubt, but now the hair was tangled from neglect. Given money and clothes, Avery would've fit in with any number of young women of the time. She probably liked music. She probably liked to dance and drink. But, although her face was scrubbed clean, the veneer of poverty marked her features. It was something Olsen couldn't quite pinpoint but that he'd seen many times. Dr. Kobel would call it bad breeding. Olsen, who'd grown up in a family without money, wasn't so sure. Personally, the idea of sterilizing such people disgusted him.

In a sense, he'd approached Avery in order to tell her this: if he'd been a decade younger, he would be in her shoes. He would have been a candidate for sterilization. She looked broken and he wanted to tell her that. He also wanted to hear her talk, though, so he held onto his thoughts. He suspected she was far from feebleminded. Her demeanor said as much. Her ability to break into the TB ward nightly said as much.

With an edge of distrust, she said, "Just come out and ask what you want to ask."

A little startled that she'd responded, he said, "Ask what exactly?"

Avery straightened. "You wanna know why I stay with Mr. Galen. Isn't that right?"

Olsen shrugged. He took a drag on the cigarette. "I'm curious," he admitted.

She shook her head. There was something very tough, very hard about her character. She was a fighter. Life was unkind to her.

"You know what they say about Galen, don't you?" he prodded. "About what he did in Indian country. He was over in the main ward before he had TB." Olsen gestured at the main building, the one with bars on the windows. "He isn't right upstairs, little miss. He isn't safe. He's got a lot of blood on his hands."

Avery stood—a gradual motion she'd been inching towards since Olsen sat. "I know what they say," she remarked. "And I know fully well *what* he is and what he's capable of." She lifted the cigarette from Olsen's hand and put it between her lips. A trickle of smoke emerged from her nose and the sensation made her grin a little. It was an odd, detached smile. She handed the cigarette back. Her fingernails were chewed to the rind. "What's your name?" she asked.

Olsen told her.

"Thanks for the smoke," she said.

Olsen nodded, taken aback. *I'll be damned,* he thought.

In the darkened room, a gymnasium at times and a dance hall and cinema at others, silver images flickered against a taut sheet on the wall: the exterior of a castle, a medieval procession, the Earl of Huntingdon on horseback. With no organist to accompany the images, the movie played in silence. A large number of patients watched with shadows on their faces. A few dozed. Dr. Brantley, who owned a collection of 16mm film prints, was screening the Douglas Fairbanks *Robin Hood* again. This and Fairbanks's *The Black Pirate* were two of his favorites, and he subjected the patients to each film quite frequently. Brantley was an enthusiast who went to see new films weekly and bought *Photoplay* off the newsstand (he had a tower of magazines in his office), but he had his comfort pictures. Presently, the face of Little John filled the screen, and a few laughs rippled through the crowd, disturbing the hush.

Like sentinels, Olsen and Mallory stood at the side of the room guarding the exit. Both men had stood and watched *Robin Hood* a dozen times, so they whispered things about Dr. Kobel and Mr. Galen and Avery Sarsfield with little attention to the show. For the non-violent patients and those who weren't quarantined with illness, attendance at the films was mandatory, and yet Avery was absent. Olsen had watched and waited for her at the door, but she was the only one of the feebleminded lot who hadn't shown.

Following a lewd suggestion about the smitten Brantley and his idol Fairbanks, Mallory proposed he and Olsen slip out the exit and have a look for the little miss. Olsen agreed. After all, it was their duty to keep tabs on the patients, and currently Avery was a no show, whereabouts unknown. The men slipped from the darkness, unnoticed by the transfixed Brantley.

A couple nurses stood in the bright hallway, laughing to themselves. One of the women, out of uniform, wore fur over her shoulders and a bell-shaped cloche over her hair. She was, it appeared, heading out for the night. She looked exquisite, with a sculpted jawline and red lips, but she had her sights on doctors rather than attendants. The nurses looked up with suspicion as Olsen and Mallory passed.

"Smoke break," Olsen explained.

The women went back to talking, uninterested.

Outside, the night was cold and damp. Trees in the courtyard swayed. Mallory watched Olsen light a cigarette, and then said, "You know why Kobel's pissed, don't you?"

Olsen, on the front steps with the gothic structure over his shoulders, looked around to see if eavesdroppers were near. He didn't trust the nurses. He saw one face above, staring downward through the bars, but it was one of the ward's severe cases, a man who couldn't repeat a coherent thought even if written down for him. Hale was his name, and he'd been locked in his room for a decade or more. He thought he was made of glass so he moved little. Olsen exhaled smoke and nodded. "Kobel's trying to work his magic," he said. "It's not working and he's jealous."

Dr. Kobel had a lascivious reputation for manipulating, sometimes even bribing, female patients to sleep with him. As a psychiatrist, he had their ear and he had tricks and he had money. He went after the sterilized girls with energy, the feebleminded ones, confident in the lack of consequences. So it was said. There were rumors amid the staff that, when his tricks failed, he forced his way with patients. No one said rape, but there it was. Kobel was arrogant enough to brag, but he wouldn't breech the subject of these illicit affairs. He talked about women he'd had outside the hospital walls but said nothing about the ones he'd taken within the walls. He never incriminated himself. He was careful and smart.

"You're damn right he's jealous," Mallory said. "You ever see him in TB before all this?"

Olsen hadn't. He worked on the Chesterfield. Kobel was a psychiatrist and nothing more. The smoke smoothed his tension.

"He goes in there just to drag her out."

"I spoke to her today," Olsen said. He'd saved this revelation. He raised his eyebrows, waiting for a reaction. Then, pleased at Mallory's curiosity, he went on. "She's not stupid. Far from it. She had a spark. Something alive."

"Yeah, well ... you know how that is. Wrong side of the tracks is all it takes with assholes like Kobel. She won't say a damn thing to me. I've tried a few times."

"When did you try?"

With a dismissive gesture, Mallory asked, "What'd she say?"

"She said she knew about Galen." Olsen crossed his arms and flicked the cigarette. Ashes spilled against the step, against his shoe. "She knows what he did in Oklahoma."

Mallory laughed, his breath a cloud of frost. He warmed his hands. "Hell, everybody knows that. It was in the news. Cold-blooded son of a bitch is what Galen is. If he'd done what he did to white folks he'd be in the electric chair, consumption or not. And if he weren't old—"

"Old or not, you're going to see Kobel slip him something if he keeps interrupting his chances. You watch."

"And if he wasn't sick," Mallory continued, "they'd put him upstairs here where he used to be." He craned his neck and looked upward to the roof where the façade ended in a toothed battlement. "Cold blooded son of a bitch."

Olsen finished the cigarette. He stomped the remains. Satisfied that no one followed them out of curiosity, he said, "Right now she's either with Galen or Kobel. Shall we find her?"

Mallory agreed.

As the attendants crossed the front drive and entered the park-like courtyard with its bed of leaves, Mallory said, "Did you get anywhere with her? She ain't bad looking. She's slender but she ain't bony. I bet she's soft, too."

"Huh?"

"Did you ask her out? You even had a picture to take her to."

"Shut the hell up. She's a kid."

"I'm just funnin'," Mallory said. "What do you care?"

"Being halfway decent, I care. That Greek to you?"

"Like in the picture, huh? You're Robin and she's Maid Marian. That it?"

"Yeah, that's it. And your waddling ass is Little John."

Mallory shrugged. "Could be worse. Kobel's the sheriff."

Olsen laughed. "Who's Galen?"

"He's King Richard. A warped King Richard."

"I see you've thought this through."

The tuberculosis ward was dark and quiet, the patients ordered to extinguish lights and go to sleep an hour prior. Olsen entered first, followed by Mallory. The cathedral radio at the front desk played music, the soft voice of a crooner over brass instruments, but the nurse on duty was nowhere in sight. Fluorescent light covered the tiled floor.

"Maybe she's with Kobel," Mallory suggested, only partly in jest. The doctor had a reputation with nurses, as well.

The music moved lightly through the corridor and stairwell. As Olsen and Mallory ascended to the second floor, the song faded, replaced by a hush. At points, the creak of a spring, a fit of coughing, and shuffling footsteps on the floor above interrupted the silence, but still there was gravity in being distant from the music. The second floor was colder than the first. The breezeway, which connected all of the patient rooms under exterior awnings on the second and third floors, allowed a draft inside the building. Only the first floor was immune to this. The rooms above were never shuttered perfectly. The rooms and hallways were always cold.

Olsen and Mallory moved toward the room of Mr. Galen, careful to make as little noise as possible. It was dark save for a small emergency light at the far end of the corridor, a red bulb that hollowed out the darkness near the ground. The men no longer spoke, afraid to wake the often fragile, geriatric patients. Vapors of ammonia hung in the air, mingling with an underlying stench of decay. The breath of TB patients smelled like rotten blood, and the tang was always present. No quantity of ammonia could erase the sickly fragrance.

The attendants stopped at Galen's door. It was a solid door with a vent for air at the bottom and nothing more. It was locked from the outside. Sharing a nod, they listened to soft voices inside: that of a young woman and that of an old man. As they had expected, Avery was here. Galen, who never said much of anything to anybody, and never had family to visit, punctuated Avery's plea with a sob of frustration. That was the first thing they heard. It was an astonishing transformation for a man who spent most of his waking hours in glacial silence, staring at a window. Audibly jarred, Galen said in a raspy voice, "He won't do it again. He'll never hurt you."

Avery whispered her gratitude, and she began to cry.

"Now, now," Galen said.

Mallory shook his head in disbelief. Olsen suppressed a nervous laugh, stilling his breath. Both men were incredulous. This was a man who, earlier in his miserable life, had—

"Sit down," Galen whispered. "Be calm. You're safe. You're safe here."

"He does the same to other girls," Avery said. "He said the state's on his side. That I'm an animal to them and no one would believe me anyway. He held me down," she started.

"I believe you," Galen said. "I've always believed you."

"He held me down. ..." Avery's voice trailed off.

Olsen, feeling the weight of the rumors about Kobel, believed her, too. He felt sick. He glanced at Mallory. He, too, had a look of horror and disgust. In the red light, he looked green. For Olsen, the dread of guilt crept in. A single thought lashed at him: he'd known about Kobel and did nothing. Suddenly, he regretted knowing the truth. He preferred the lack of responsibility that went with rumors.

Then a duo of noises came through the door that stopped both attendants cold: the click of a bullet entering the cylinder of a revolver, and the spin of the cylinder into place.

"Where'd she get a gun?" Mallory whispered. Something in him changed. The words spilled out, panicked.

Olsen shook his head tightly. *Don't speak*, he thought. He wanted to strangle Mallory then and there.

"Where'd she get a gun?" Mallory said, now louder, as if he wanted to be heard. He might as well have flooded the ward with light.

*It's not us they're after,* Olsen thought. He made emphatic gestures for Mallory to be silent. *It's Kobel. Stay out of it. It's Kobel. Not us.*

Mallory slammed his fist against the metal door, trembling it. "What's going on in there?" he said.

*Jesus Christ,* Olsen thought, backing away. The retreat was instinctive. Mallory was possessed.

The commotion brought other patients from their sleep. Confused murmuring issued from the room next to Galen's. Other voices spilled into the corridor.

Galen and Avery were silent then.

"What are you doing?" Olsen asked. In his mind, he still had the hope of grabbing Mallory by the arm and dragging him towards the stairs. He balled his fist in preparation. Even if it cost him his job, he was prepared to drag him down the stairs and kick his head in. Why would Mallory be concerned about protecting a guy like Kobel? He despised Kobel. His shock turned to anger at Mallory's stupidity.

Mallory lifted a key from his belt and slid it into the door.

Olsen took another step back. The stairwell, at the opposite end of the hall, felt very distant. He was backing into a wall.

The door opened and Mallory filled the void. "Hand over the gun," he ordered. "Hand it over or you're gonna get more of the same, little miss."

A tick of silence passed. Then, emphatically, Avery said, "That's him! That's him, that's him."

"That's not Doc Kobel!" Olsen shouted.

Mallory started forward, lunging.

The shot was a flash of light in the darkness of the room. Mallory's heavy body slammed against the floor a second later.

When the police climbed the stairs, Olsen was sitting in the reception area with a blanket over his shoulders. The radio still played. He fumbled with a cigarette, trying to light it with his shaking fingers. He was unsuccessful.

Dr. Kobel, a slender man with a smudge of mustache, stood at his side. He struck a match on the desk and lit Olsen's cigarette. Again, he asked, "You're sure Galen was alone? You're certain Ms. Sarsfield wasn't with him? Is that really your story, Olsen?"

Olsen inhaled. He shook his head. "She wasn't there," he muttered.

"The cops won't like having to stitch together how an invalid got his hands on a gun. Somebody had to bring it to him. They might even look at you. You prepared for that?"

"Galen can talk, can't he? If he says he was alone, then he was alone."

Kobel stared for a moment. "Yes, he can talk. Listen, I thought you were Mallory's pal. Well he's dead up there now. You realize that, don't you? His brain's coming out his nose. It's on the floor. You too shocked to realize that, Olsen? Mallory's dead."

Olsen nodded. "I saw," he muttered. He had, regrettably, looked.

Kobel switched off the radio, frustrated, a little scared. The voices faded. Perhaps he knew about Mallory. Maybe the two were in competition. "Get some fresh air and clear your mind. They'll want to talk to you." Then, shaking his head, Dr. Kobel started towards the stairs. Dr. Mundy, impatient, had called to him from the stairwell.

Olsen passed a cop on the front steps. He warned Olsen not to go far. Olsen pointed to a bench in the courtyard near a sassafras tree, just beyond the amassed crowd of patients, attendants, nurses, and doctors. "I'll be there," he said. "I'll wait."

The cop nodded. "Guess this is a hazard of the job," the man added. He was an old cop; he'd seen it all and had taken it in stride. Nothing alarmed him. That line—hazard of the job—would make it to the papers probably and soon that line would be the long and short of it: attendant James Mallory died in the line of duty. He gave his all helping the feebleminded and infirm. Such is life. A hero? Possibly. Galen was certainly a villain, despite the act of chivalry. What Mallory did to Avery Sarsfield, and what Kobel was possibly still doing, didn't matter. A detail like that wouldn't surface.

Olsen shrugged. *Such is life* summed it up better than anything. He worked through the crowd, ghostly enough that no one bothered him with questions. That would come later. A bounty of attention, good and bad, awaited him. He'd have to lie.

He hoped Avery would be at the bench but, of course, she was not there. She was too smart. She had everything covered, he guessed. She feigned sleep in her ward or maybe she hid in the crowd. Perhaps, even now, she watched him.

He'd nearly grabbed her as she stepped over Mallory's sprawled body and started down the hall. She left Galen behind with a gun in his hands. Galen was willing to do that for her, to remain alone and take sole blame.

*That wasn't Kobel,* Olsen had said, mortified. *That was Mallory. That's Jimmy Mallory. He was an attendant. He didn't—.* He'd been in shock, rambling, confused. He'd only seen old people die before. He'd never seen blood like that. And there was a lot of blood. Mallory had died so quickly. He'd been alive and then he wasn't. God, it was a crushing thing to witness.

Avery had stood there as if she were contemplating fallen leaves. She had, he noticed then, eyes like opaque glass. He couldn't fathom what went on behind them, if there was guilt or just anger. *I know exactly who Mallory is*, she had said.

Then it dawned on him. He'd been so set on Kobel he couldn't imagine Mallory being a culprit. *He did it to other girls, too.* He felt sick and wondered what Avery thought of his connection to Mallory. He'd thought of the man as a friend. He had no idea. *Are you going to kill me, too, then?* he'd asked, uncertain of the depths of her anger.

*You were kind to me*, Avery said. With that, she was gone, sprinting towards the stairs. Presumably she'd slipped out unseen, under cover of music in the empty reception area.

He thought, *You were kind to me and it'll pay to continue being kind to me.*

Olsen took a seat on the cold bench and worked on his cigarette. He pulled the blanket closer, shivering. *Feeblemindedness,* he thought. *She's going to get away with murder. Her hands are clean.* He understood why Kobel had that scared look in his eyes, and why he wanted Olsen to name Avery. Obstinately, he thought, *I'm not going to do it. You're on your own, Doc.*

# SIR OXNARD

## Jeffrey Hunt

Sir Oxnard returned, and to little fanfare.

Though he quickly became the talk of the town. Or countryside, really, as only plebeians live within city limits. You're a commoner if you can see another house from your own, and a lout if you share a street—or at least that was the view in Cheshire County, where Sir Oxnard was born and raised. And after twelve years away, he was back.

The family had said Sir Oxnard was "temporarily absent," "momentarily away," or was "taking an extended holiday." Though truth be told, Sir Oxnard was run off. His speech never fit with those around him, and his decorum was not up to standard. Sir Oxnard cussed and spit. His hygiene, at best, was just adequate. He loved the type of sports that got one dirty and caused people to yell. But worst of all, he lived for jokes.

Clean humor, dirty humor, horrible puns, and Sir Oxnard wasn't above religious jabs, either. "Have you heard the one about the pregnant nun?" he asked the priest, loudly, during a holy moment of silence, which was the second-to-the-last straw. The last came when Sir Oxnard set his uncle's summer house on fire, making his aunt think her husband had perished. Though truly, the Baron was passed out safe and sound in the outbuilding, the victim of laxative-laced cake his nephew had gifted him the night before. It was double demonstration of Sir Oxnard's favorite type of joke—the practical one.

And for his family that incident was a bridge too far.

"He has to go," said Sir Oxnard's mother. She was emphatic, though somewhat hard to take seriously, as her wig was pink.

"Agreed," said Sir Oxnard's father. His undershirt, as well as the rest of his clothes, had been dyed, too.

"Banish him from Cheshire County!"

"No, let's send him out of the country!"

"Or kill him!" said Sir Oxnard's sister. She was the only one not in pink; her wardrobe had been turned purple.

"Will the Duke help?"

"In driving him away?"

"Or in killing him?"

"With both, probably."

"But do we want to go that far?"

"I think so," Sir Oxnard's sister stated. Though she was unsurprised when her parents opted for the more genteel option.

So they enlisted the help of the Duke, Sir Herbert Cheshire, of whom the county was named, and Sir Oxnard was forced away. And it was to much of the nobility's pleasure. No more jokes about one's mums and dads. No more fingers pointed to long noses, and comparisons made to elephants, no more advertisements in papers for erectile dysfunction cures with testimonials signed by real-life county residents. No more roads closed due to snow in July, or town squares sold to foreigners for pennies, or candied absinthe given to entire Kindergarten classes. Sir Oxnard put up a fight—forced from his home and his friends—but Duke Herbert was more powerful. So everyone got to tell Sir Oxnard "hard cheese," that quintessential English expression for "bad luck," and that was that.

Was it fair? Did he deserve it?

A few said Sir Oxnard never hurt anyone—he was removed due to his impropriety, not due to any danger he posed. And was it humane to let Sir Oxnard's numerous ant colonies die, even if they were just kept to be stuck in people's slacks? Or to turn all of his cats out? What had the cats done to deserve a hard life in the wild, other than unknowingly supply Sir Oxnard with urine to be put in women's perfume bottles? Though Sir Oxnard really should have heeded the warnings, they all agreed, so again "hard cheese" and there was nothing more to be said.

Until Sir Herbert passed away, that is.

And with him went the power to keep Sir Oxnard away.

Nothing happens for a year.

"I thought he was back?" they all ask in their shacks.

"Did the man return or not?" they wonder in their shanties and country huts. And there's hardly any worry in their voices, because after all, what's not to like about a crazed nobleman with means? A hearty bit of entertainment he used to provide, and many of the high schoolers have fond memories of their visit with the green fairy so many years before, courtesy of Cheshire County's number-one trickster.

But in their estates and mansions and country manners the terror which couches similar questions is palatable.

The occasional sighting at the lake or on forest trails eventually convinces most that Sir Oxnard has indeed returned, and then after a year, invitations go out. The entire upper crust of Cheshire County is called to Sir Oxnard's newly-completed palazzo for a dinner party, to celebrate the one-year anniversary of his return. The cards explain that the residence is outfitted with all the "finest amenities wealth can afford," on grounds which have been planted and landscaped "with every detail considered and with every stone over-turned," and that there will be food which can only be described as "divine." It will be reformation celebration, a showing of amends, and please, won't they all attend?

Of course, everyone's suspicious.

"It's a trap!" Sir Oxnard's sister declares.

"He's going to set roaches on me again," says Lady Durham.

"Or steal my dentures!" yells Sir Devon.

"Remember when he rented all my rooms to the Romani?"

"Not as bad as when he replanted all of my trees upside-down, on the entirety of my 600 acres!"

"He petitioned the MP on my behalf, regarding suffrage for the dead!" screams the Baroness. "When I thought poor Henry was gone for the first time in that fire!"

Yet despite it all, social rules dictated they must attend. Perhaps Sir Oxnard has changed, and truth be told, they all want to see his new palazzo. And they will be cautious. So on the instructed night they arrive in their carriages, and perfectly mannerly and sharply-dressed butlers and maids greet them at the front drive, take their coats, give them hors d'oeuvres, serve them up bubbling flutes. The guests are hesitant—and especially the late Sir Herbert's son and grandson, both named after their forbearer, of course—but the canapés are exquisite, the spanakopita the most delicate they've ever had, and the wine is certified from the *Vallée de la Marne*, or "champagne valley" in France, and made from grapes grown and fermented to standards unchanged for centuries on end.

And the décor! The live concerto! The silverware and gilded plates! The ten full courses! "My sincerest and deepest apologies," says the humble, and now seemingly utterly pleasant, host. And as he bows to all, he doesn't even crack a smirk. Rumor has it he's spent the last dozen years in The Rhineland, where they don't take kindly to humor, though others say he'd been in the New World. And still others whisper he'd been set to manual labor! But whatever the terms of his exile, and whatever he's been up to while away, Sir Oxnard has apparently changed.

The man's quick to eat and drink with them, so no reason not to try his offerings. In the dining room they check beneath the table for snakes or hounds, but it's all on the up-and-up. The musicians don't break into boorish flamencos, and there isn't an insult or shaggy dog joke to be heard. Instead, Sir Oxnard spends the evening apologizing, to each and every guest, with great specificity and sincerity. And four hours in, not only is every invitee still in attendance, but they're all having a certifiable time! "If only Sir Herb had passed away sooner!" some whisper, and though the thought is uncouth—they're all in their cups, of course—it's true!

In the fifth hour, as the clock strikes midnight, Sir Oxnard has loosened and is telling stories. But they're tales about percentages and getting income from land, about purchasing livestock and indentured contracts, about winning and losing at horse tracks—proper types of conversation! Then at one in the morning, with all still present, he takes the pince-nez off his nose, lights a pipe, and mentions that to replace his penchant for philistine joviality, he's "taken up cheese."

"Buying, selling, making, aging," Sir Oxnard explains.

"Any particular type?" Sir Herbert II asks.

"Oh, anything and everything," Sir Oxnard replies.

And really, it's all quite interesting.

"Camembert?"

"I have thirty stone!"

"Asiago?"

"One hundred stone!"

"Manchego?"

"None at the moment, properly speaking. But when it finishes curdling next week, I'll have enough to fill this room!"

And this goes on; conversation about creamy emmentals, and crumbly stiltons, and the profits that can be made exporting Edams. Until finally, Sir Oxnard asks if his guests would like a tour of his stores on the lower floors. And the bottom of the palazzo is a marvel, of vats and drying racks! The front of the first sub-basement is stacked with golden yellow roquefots and muensters. The next sub-basement has only Ädelost—on account of the aroma—but the one below has mascarpone and manouri and the sweetest pecorino Sir Oxnard's guests have ever tasted. They go through four more equally wondrous storerooms of resting and ripening dairy, and then come to a padlocked door.

"Now, would you like to see my personal collection?"

Everyone assents, and loudest of all is Sir Herb III, who can't for the life of him understand what beef this wonderful man and his grandfather had. But most importantly, what could possibly be in Sir Oxnard's locked-away compartments, after all the other gustatory marvels they've just seen and sampled?

They continue to insist, so Sir Oxnard takes a key from a loop around his neck.

He opens the padlock.

And they rush inside.

The first private room contains abertam, but of a variety they've never experienced. Sir Oxnard takes out his pince-nez and places them back on his nose. He reads a label on one of the nearest wheels: "From the Czech countryside, outside Karlovy Vary. Made of sheep's milk, with completely natural orange coloring—no annatto added, or anything else. So it's just like how cheese should be: pure. And aged twelve years."

The guests "ooh" and "aah," and after Sir Oxnard cuts into the circle of completely unadulterated curd they take samples aplenty. Then it's to the next door, in the back of the room.

Which has two padlocks.

Sir Oxnard takes two keys from inside his vest pocket. He unlocks, then opens the door, and the country nobility run inside once more. "*Afuega'l pitu*, from the Principality of Asturias," reads Sir Oxnard. "One of the oldest cheeses on the continent, and completely unpasteurized. As pure as the last cheese, with just milk, salt, and rennet, and recognized by the *Denominación de Origen* as a national treasure. Aged fifteen years and then delivered straight here."

"This *is* divine!" exclaims Sir Oxnard's sister.

"Never in my life!" yells the Baroness, and from the look of joy on her face it's clear all sins have been forgiven.

"Enjoy," says Sir Oxnard.

"We will! We will!" Cheshire County's best shout back.

They consume the cheese until they are nearly splitting, then they lean against the wooden cheese boxes, stacked from stone floor to timbered ceiling. Until after a while, someone notices three padlocks glimmering in the light of the torches further back. The door is small, and made of dark wood, held together with thick metal beams set on black hinges. "What's behind there?" they ask.

"Oh, just ... my *absolute* pride and joy."

"Which is?"

"Tell us!"

"You wouldn't possibly be interested."

"We are, we are!"

Sir Oxnard takes off his pince-nez, scratches his nose, and laughs. "But you're all so stuffed!"

"We have room! Open it! Just a little more!"

Sir Oxnard places his pince-nez back on. "Very well." He unhooks a chain tied around his ankle. He lifts up three keys. He unlocks each of the three padlocks.

And as they push him out of the way, he smiles.

The cheeses thus far have been so fantastic, so perfect, so *heavenly!* And despite being full, well as they say, isn't there always room for Jarlsberg? The guests fight and squeeze, and when the room opens after several body lengths it's like a cork from a bottle. *Splash!* Down they go into a pit of thick and utterly vile black liquid.

Is it molasses?

Is it oil?

It's more putrid than both, and too chunky to be sewage, with dark floating abscesses that break open as the guests thrash about. *Splash! Splash!* They keep running forward and falling down and in, driven to the muck by people pushing from behind. *Splash! Splash! Splash!* And without a single torch to warn them of what's ahead, they're utterly helpless!

"Sir Oxnard, Sir—*cough, cough*! What *is* this?"

"The aroma!" *Cough!*

*Cough!* "The smell!" *Gag!*

*Cough! Gag!* "I can't touch the bottom!" *Retch!* "And I can't get out!" The last is one of the Herbs, but it's impossible to tell which—the foul tar renders everyone the same.

They're all sputtering now, and hacking, and a guest outright vomits. It turns into a chain reaction, and truly, the reappearance of everything Cheshire County's best have enjoyed the past evening only improves the black liquid they're treading in—it's that abominable. A duchess finds and tries scaling the steps to get out of the pit, and she's almost to Sir Oxnard, who stands above. But then she succumbs to her stomach, and as she too hurls up her meal, she spasms and slips back into the mire with a terrific splatter. And Sir Oxnard now all-out grins.

"Why, you're all so stuffed you can barely swim!" he says.

"Save us, save us from this!" they scream.

"Well get stuffed!" Sir Oxnard yells, and turns away.

Clearly this is revenge for his exile, some guests realize. No one has mind enough ask what it is they're bobbing and throwing up and covered in, and many start to choke and drown.

Sir Oxnard walks away, continuing to smile until he reaches the opening of the cellar on the other side of the wall. Then he calls back, "Why members of the upper crust, I can think of nothing better than serving YOU some cottage cheese!" His eyes burn red behind his pince-nez, like the wax on a finely preserved loaf of cheddar, as he locks the door behind him. And now Sir Oxnard can shout the lines he's long waited to say: "Two tons, un-pressed and un-pasteurized! Made with milk from English Herefords, brought from all over this very county!"

"Have mercy!" they cry through the door. "Get us out!"

But Sir Oxnard ignores them.

"Soft cheese, ha ha! Soft cheese is what you're in! But I think it's rather *hard cheese* too, isn't it?"

"We're dying—*Cough! Gag! Retch!*—this is torture!"

"Hard cheese that I brought in on the very first day of my return, so it's AGED FOR TWELVE WHOLE MONTHS!" And then, after a whispered "enjoy," he leaves.

Sir Oxnard re-padlocks the next two doors, then ascends to his bedroom. Once inside he pours himself a bourbon, and as he sips his drink, he contemplates how despite always looking down on things like Pepper Jack or Kaukauna or those flavorless cream balls covered in almonds you see at parties, there actually might be something to dairy with spices and other added flavorings. And though Sir Oxnard's aged cottage cheese started off nauseating, considering the inclusion of Cheshire County's best—and with alcohol-soaked Herbs to boot—in addition to the added sweetness of revenge, the vat at the bottom of his palazzo now might truly hold the very best cheese he or anyone else has ever collected.

# SCREEN SHOT

## Teel James Glenn

Two words that seem to go together are Hollywood and irony. I point to the fact that I had to do what they call a 'psychological autopsy,' which is when you try to figure out what went through someone's mind before they put a bullet in it with out having the body to examine. After all, in this case there was no doubt about the cause of death, so all that was left was the reason.

"I can't make sense of any of it," the now-dead space captain said on the laptop screen. Behind him was a calendar with half the dates X-ed out in blood red and a rack of hats on a wall, a very non-spaceship setting. "I have to end it," he continued. Then the image of the man on the screen put the revolver in his hand up to his right temple and pulled the trigger.

I froze the screen before his falling forward onto the laptop had shut it off. And before he'd splattered his brains out of the side of his head. I turned to the woman who had brought the thumb drive with the gruesome image to me. "I've looked at this a number of times since I got this, Mrs. Barnet, and I can't think any differently than the police; your brother killed himself and this video proves it."

The middle-aged woman that sat across from me in the booth at Universal Studio's café was clearly past tears, but the aura of misery hung around her like a cloud. "I know that, Mister Shadows," she said, "but despite what the public thought, my brother was a deeply religious man, a devout Catholic and his taking his own life like this ... was ... was an aberration. I know he has had periods of deep depression but to think that something drove him to this, and I missed it, is a guilt I cannot live with. What could have caused such desperation, such depths of pain? I want to know; I need to know if there is something I could have done."

I was in Los Angeles on another case when the Shadows Foundation coordinator referred Jill Barnet to me. I really didn't see I could do anything but agree with the police's final ruling on the suicide of Bill Shaker, famous for the Role of Space Captain Cody in the '90s TV series. He was in the process of making the revival movie when, on a lunch break, he put a gun to his head.

I had enjoyed his show way back when, and to see him—in his captain's uniform—put that gun to his head was startling even to this jaded investigator. I guess you could say his last show was his most spectacular.

"I don't know that I can do much to give you the closure you want, Mrs. Barnet. It is all pretty cut and dried."

"That's what they say, Mister Shadows, but it's not true. Why? I have to know why. I have nowhere else to go."

There it was, the appeal. The mandate of the Foundation was "*Help for the helpless, hope for the hopeless,*" so I could not really turn my back on her; even if I could only give her a vague peace of mind, I had to try.

"Okay," I said, "I will look into it."

The first thing I wanted to do was get a sense of who the man was, in order to find out what could have driven him to suicide. I started at where it ended for him, his bungalow on the Universal lot.

It was an odd feeling walking down those back-lot streets in the off hours, the New York Street so familiar from so many movies, and the European street right next to it. I was impressed especially by the cobbled stones under the arch where the Frankenstein monster had raged against the villagers so long ago.

Hollywood magic seemed so real walking on those streets, but then, that was the whole idea.

The little bungalow was in a line of others and still had the 'do not enter' tape across the door. I had written authorization and a key so I went in.

Inside the room had been untouched from the day, two weeks ago, when William 'Bill' John Shaker had been found with his brains blown out on the floor of the room.

Once the door was closed, all outside sound was gone and I was alone as he must have been in those last moments.

I stood for a moment to take it in.

To my right was the big production calendar with all but the last two days crossed off; a hat rack with several fedoras that he favored and was known for wearing; and an open closet with spare uniforms, a suit jacket, robe and slippers. Next to it was a bathroom door.

To my left was a daybed under a long, high-up window with some photos on the wall of Shaker from various series he had been in; *RD Walker-Police*, *The Barberry War* and, of course, *Space Captain Cody* (from his two-year run in the early '90s).

Straight ahead was the desk with a makeup mirror above it with photos and notes stuck up on the glass. I found myself looking at me standing there at the door and thought I looked a bit lost for what to do next.

On the floor was a dark stain in the carpet that was evidence of the last moments of the actor Bill Shaker, whose histrionic performances I had enjoyed as Space Captain Cody.

I crossed the room and pulled up the rattan chair to the desk to sit down. His laptop computer had been on the desk in front of me.

I looked at the mementos around the mirror. There were a number of snapshots: Shaker and his sister at some premier years ago, one of his racehorses, his estranged wife from better days when she had first guest starred on his old show. Tucked among them were a Catholic mass card for another actor who had passed away two years ago, and some cartoon drawings of his Captain Cody character from some fan of the original show. And a rosary.

I put my hand on the desk, trying to imagine his headspace before he put the gun to his temple.

In the mirror I could see what I had in the video with the hat rack and calendar, the light streaming in from the window.

None of it made sense; he had done two seasons of a show that a short-lived network canceled, but it wasn't the end of a career. He'd had work before and work since—a steady, if unremarkable leading TV actor's career. And in the recent years, cable and streaming reruns of the show had made it a cult hit. Shaker had, in the meantime, bought the rights to the character and so jumped on producing and starring in a revival TV film with hopes for a series.

"No sense at all," I said looking once more around the room. "You should have been on top of the world, Captain Cody!"

"Bill was a freaking religious nut." Gloria La Mar was every bit a Hollywood ex-wife with more man-made parts than a Tesla but her anger at Shaker was real. "He kept saying he couldn't divorce me because it was a sin!"

She had agreed to meet me in a diner on Cahuenga Boulevard and had entered the place like she was walking the red carpet. I recognized her from an old episode of *Space Captain Cody*, though I suspected back then there had been more original parts. I couldn't tell if she was smiling or was stuck in a stiff wind because the skin on her face was so tight.

"So, you're saying you can't believe he would take his own life?"

"Well, he would go to mass five times a week and all that," she said with disgust, "but it still didn't stop him from breaking his wedding vows by sharing his Captain's log with little fangirls at conventions."

"Is that why you left him?"

"Those little flakes were barely a blip," she laughed. "They could never give a man what I could." I thought I saw the memory of an expression on her face. "I tried for a long time to be what he wanted, to stay young for him; it didn't matter. Ultimately though, I left him because I found a better man who loves me for who I really am. That simple. But Bill had to be in control, he would not let me go; would not let me marry the love of my life."

I tried to figure if she was playing me, but her statement rang as the only real thing about her. I had to press on. "Can you think of anything, anything at all that might have driven him to this?"

She shook her head and I thought I caught some real expression under the flesh mask, almost sadness. "I wanted to be free, just not this way."

"Bill Shaker was a shit," Jeffery Matthews said. "When I found him dead in his dressing room it just proved what an arrogant, self-serving prig he was. Whatever made him check out, he didn't give a damn about me or the rest of the production group." Matthews was a thin man, but not a frail one, with long-fingered hands that were those of an artist. He was seated in his office a few blocks from Universal Studios, surrounded by models of spaceships from *Space Captain Cody* and several other shows he had worked on as special effects supervisor.

"You don't mince words, Mister Matthews," I said. He'd been gracious enough about seeing me but made sure I was not there for any kind of 'on the record' comment.

"Don't get me wrong," he added, "on screen he held the eye and he knew Cody; I really do think he would have made this revival a real hit."

"But?"

"But as a human being he was almost the opposite of that caring, connecting character. He was a people user—could never allow anyone else to have the spotlight; not his co-stars, his wives, his friends. And he was vicious in business."

"Yet you were co-producer on this revival with him; you co-wrote it."

He shrugged. "I fleshed out his script idea, yes, but be clear there was no show without him. And he knew there was no show without me; I started in the old show as physical props and rose to SFX supervisor but a lot of the 'in' stuff in the old show came out of my innovations, even if he refused to acknowledge them then. He realized this by this incarnation, which is why he came to me. And there was no way this one would look as good for the budget we were able to raise, without me." He pointed to a screen on the wall with footage running of the revival show—what they call raw footage. There were a series of numbers running across the bottom of the screen.

There was no sound but images of Shaker, in character, striding around the command deck of his spaceship. The scene shifted to what looked like a planet surface with several of the other crewmembers trudging across a hostile landscape. One of the space-suited figures stumbled and the picture froze.

"Okay, Doug," Matthews said into a recorder he held up to his face. "At 21:27 the shadows are not tracking on the planet surface. Fix them."

I looked at the screen and sure enough, now that he mentioned it the shadows cast by the two astronauts did not match those of the rocks they were maneuvering through. When Matthews saw my expression he said, "CGI sets, the whole planet surface is provided via green screen. It allows us to put in the backgrounds. Only way we could afford the scope of the script."

"Movie magic," I said.

"TV budget magic," he laughed. Then his expression got serious. "And thank God for it, it was the only way we could write around Shaker offing himself."

"How so?"

"The last two days were planned to be shoots of the planet surface and his character was supposed to be in it. They were key to the story and were spread through the script. We were able to use a double for all the suit shots with a little rewriting, use an old close-up of him, and put it in the helmet for the last shot. We gave all the lines to other actors and you just see him smiling. I'll show you—" He touched a button on the desk and forwarded the footage on the screen to a shot of a space suited figure standing alone against a fictional vista. The camera zoomed in and the last shot was a smiling Bill Shaker inside that suit.

"Wow," I said. "Sure looks real."

"Yes, it does," he beamed. "I'm good at what I do. That will give us an ending that works for this show. No thanks to Shaker. We had to take three days off after he died and then a number of skull sessions to figure this ending that works. Another full week for me to get the effect. But it works, in fact I think it works better than what we had."

"So, can you think why he would do it? Why would he kill himself?"

"Pure meanness?" he said quickly with bitterness in his voice. "If he killed himself, we could not use any insurance to finish the film; if I hadn't figured how to save it with the footage and give some of his lines to the first officer and other actors,

I would have been out a lot."

"You have investment in it?"

"He came to me with it. I mortgaged my home to get this going, took out a loan, found other investors. He did nothing but complain; said there was no picture without him, that he would 'save' my failed career." He stepped up from out behind his desk, now agitated. "Like any of his shows had been a runaway success? I was making a living; I'm the one who hadn't blown all my money on hair-brain schemes and still had a home to mortgage."

"He wasn't wise in his investments?"

"He was an idiot at anything but looking good on camera. Oh, he could negotiate like a wolf but then his lack of discipline would make it fail. At least he was too stupid to ruin me completely by waiting until only two days before wrap to kill himself."

"So, you think that is why he killed himself?"

Matthews shrugged again. "I couldn't say, but if he had even done it the day before I would have lost everything."

My next stop was one of Shaker's co-stars—the only other cast member from the original run, Robert Saito, who now played First Officer Oki.

He had been one of the youngest of the cast in the original run of the show as a helmsman and had been upgraded to first officer when they brought him back. He had also been upgraded to sleeping with Gloria La Mar and was apparently the 'love of her life' she had spoken of.

He was a vital decade and a half younger than Shaker—and of Gloria's original parts, though lots of her was definitely younger than he was.

"He did everything he could to keep me from being written into the new film after he found out Gloria and I were an item," Saito said. "But fan reaction to the announcement that I was in the show at all was so overwhelming that Bill had to let them write a part for me."

He was in a dressing room on the Universal lot while on break from the legal thriller TV show he was guest starring on as the killer. "Bill and I had minimal contact, only two actual scenes together, so it wasn't too bad. Then when he … well, after he was dead, they shot a couple of new scenes with me to fill in plot stuff and gave me some of his final lines and my part really got bigger." He was combing his hair and getting ready to go back on camera. "So now, if the movie does well, they may do a spinoff with me. I guess I get the last laugh."

He rose and adjusted his tie. "Now I get his cast-off series and the wife he could not see for his own ego." He walked to the door of the room then stopped and turned to look at me in a gesture that was both dramatic and sincere at once. "Gloria is the most real person I've ever met in this fake town; I have no idea what went through Bill Shaker's mind but I'm glad he is gone, if only for leaving us free to wed."

There was not much more to press from him as he clearly was what old Perry Mason episodes would call a 'hostile witness.'

I left him and walked back over to Shaker's bungalow with no more of a clue as to what I was going to tell Jill Barnet. I had talked to a dozen more people about Bill Shaker and his state of mind and had no more idea why he would have killed himself than I had at the beginning of it all. It seemed like his career was going to take an uptick; his doctor said he had no particular sickness to be afraid of.

The director of photography had said Shaker really was beginning to show his age on camera, so lighting and angles had become much more important to maintain his 'hero status.' Could that and the fact that he had lost his wife to a younger man be enough to send him into one of his spirals of depression?

I sat in the chair he had died in and looked around the room again. "Why did you do it, Bill? Why did you leave it?"

I opened my own laptop, set it on the spot where his had been and pulled up some old episodes of *Space Captain Cody*. It was not as much fun as when I first saw them, but then what is? And with the knowledge that Cody was done and gone.

But they were still good and on-screen Bill Shaker was every bit the hero. I could see the budget limitation at this point, with none of the vast backgrounds that I had seen in Matthew's office. The cramped wooden, fake rock sets were pretty obvious. Even campy.

The Captain would make pronouncements as he tried to make sense of the week's problems, save the day and often get the alien gal. Good campy fun.

But not so for me anymore. What could I tell Jill Barnet?

I looked up around the bungalow again, over at the hat rack and the calendar with the shoot days X-ed out and suddenly I knew. I *could* make sense of it!

I just had to do some research but I was pretty sure I knew the reason that Bill Shaker died—and it was not what people thought.

There was a small premier screening of the finished *Return of Captain Cody* three weeks later in a screening room on the Universal lot. The network executives and most of the key crew of the film were there, along with Jill Barnet and myself.

First officer actor Robert Saito basked in both the praise of the executives and in the wide-eyed adoration of Gloria La Mar, who came on his arm and stayed glued to him the whole time.

Producer-writer SFX master Jeffery Matthews was glowing with praise. When the lights came up on the final scene of Space Captain Cody standing on the planet surface and smiling, the applause was thunderous.

Jill was crying with seeing her brother on the screen but they were tears of pride as well as nostalgia.

"I just wish I knew why he did it," she said as we stood near the doorway as people filed out. The principals all gathered at the back of the room for a group photo.

That was when I told her. "He didn't," I said.

The conversation around us suddenly went silent and all eyes turned to me.

"What are you talking about?" Saito asked.

"Yes," Matthews said. "What kind of nonsense are you saying?"

"Well," I said, "let's go backwards. The phrases that Shaker said in the video, "*I can't make sense of any of it*," and "*I have to end it*," were both things Space Captain Cody said in different episodes of the old series. Just innocuous phrases strung together."

"So?" Gloria said. "He was always quoting himself; like they were important famous people quotes."

I had to laugh at that. "Well, maybe, but for a self-send-off he would have chosen better; but to continue. The conversation I had with you, Mister Matthews, talking about the shadows on the TV show got me thinking, so I rewatched the suicide video again and again."

"Ghoul!" Matthews said, but there was something in his eyes beyond disgust.

"Well, the shadows were right," I continued. "They were right for that room at that time of day and that is where you foxed me. You didn't change the background like in the space scenes."

"Of all the—" he began but there was fear in his eyes now and he was assessing those around us who had shifted their gaze from me to him.

"You only changed the foreground. And that was your mistake; you took almost a week to get the Deep Fake technology right after you sat in that chair in his uniform at a lunch break and recorded yourself. You were able to substitute his face and used lines from those old episodes so the voiceprint would match his real voice. But you did sloppy work. That calendar in the background still had eight days to shoot, not the two left when he supposedly killed himself."

He started to edge toward the door but I physically blocked him and he didn't want to go against me. He still thought he could talk his way out.

So, I kept on with my explanation. "For the actual murder you went back to your roots in physical props, Matthews; you walked right up to him and put the small caliber gun to the guy's temple and pulled the trigger. He had no chance. Afterward you put a blank in the gun, pressed it into his dead hand and fired it to make sure the powder residue would read right. That bungalow was pretty soundproof and his skull muffled the full load bullet that killed him. You loaded the fake shooting on his laptop from a thumb drive to make it look like he'd done it himself and videoed it."

"You're out of your mind!" His voice cracked. He was not a quarter the actor that Shaker had been.

"Maybe," I said, "but they have forensic computer people who, now that they have a reason to, will take that video apart pixel by pixel. You have the skill and the equipment and the reason to want the whole enchilada; no reason to share with a has-been actor, right? And only you knew when you could kill him and still make the film work. How long had you planned it? From when you first wrote the script?"

He broke then and tried to run but a simple right cross took him down.

There it was. Done.

So, Hollywood and irony; Jill got the odd comfort in knowing her brother was murdered, Matthews made the revival film of Space Captain Cody a hit by the rewrite and the publicity about his being charged with the murder, and thus made Shaker a true Hollywood immortal. The new fake captain and the very real cougar's relationship seemed to be the only genuine thing I had encountered in the whole affair.

Hollywood, go figure ...

# SETTING THE PICK

## April Kelly

Here's what Dapper Donny saw when I walked into his bar: a guy a few birthday cakes north of forty, with thinning hair, a slight limp in his left leg, and a suit straight out of a Motel 6 lost and found.

His nod and my request for a scotch were perfunctory, as I heaved myself onto a stool with a weary sigh. The line of sight between my seating choice and the wall-mounted security camera in the corner above the end of the bar was direct and unimpeded. Hey, if I'm doing a screen test, I want the video to capture every detail, from the spare tire straining my worn shirt's buttons to the fine veins road mapping the mushrooming tip of a drinker's nose.

Strictly transactional, the dealings between Donny and me that first night three weeks ago, though when I laid down a twenty for a pair of four-buck pops and eased off the stool to indicate I wasn't looking for change, Donny tacked on a quick thank-you smile to his good-night nod.

Memory of the hefty tip triggered a more welcoming greeting the next evening, when I returned wearing the same shabby suit and a fresh, threadbare shirt.

"Scotch neat, right?" he asked, as I parked my can on the stool I'd claimed the night before.

"Yeah, and don't let it die of loneliness."

"Copy that."

He poured heavy, a liquid bet that the previous tip hadn't been a fluke, although I could almost hear his brain cogs grinding as he weighed my down-on-his-luck look against the size of the gratuity. Maybe he thought I had mistaken a twenty for a ten last night, but he owned the place and could pour lavish or stingy, his call.

You can only truly begin working a mark when he believes he's working you, so I waited patiently for Donny to push out a pawn. As he slid a cardboard coaster in front of me and set the squat glass on it, he didn't disappoint.

"Tough day?"

"I've had better," I said. "But then, I've also had worse."

"I hear you, brother."

Clichés being the optimum bedrock on which to build a superficial connection, I stuck to the tried and true by design. Donny, I suspected, spoke fluent bullshit because his IQ was roughly the overnight low at the Phoenix airport in August.

His full name was Donald Tucker Raffin, and once upon a time he'd been a basketball star at a high school almost three thousand miles west of the Baltimore dive in which I methodically downed a scotch many tiers below Glenfiddich, the aged-in-Caribbean-rum-casks single malt I prefer. Dapper Donny's house pour had more likely been aged in the hubcap of a Kia.

I knew all there was to know about my host, including the origin of his long-ago nickname. When he wasn't putting points on the board, eighteen-year-old Donald Raffin had dressed like a GQ model and swaggered through Jackson County High as though each corridor were a runway. He had all the markers for success—rich parents, only child, special skill set—but like many a blazing, teen comet, Don's adult iteration had fizzled into obscurity.

He blamed a run-in with the law his senior year for the short-circuiting of his basketball future, which, in his imagination, included a scholarship to a prestige university, a brilliant pro career, and million-dollar endorsement deals. That "run-in" was the murder of Tina Kemp, a crime for which Donny had been the prime suspect.

I've screened the game tapes and, truth be told, his basketball skills were only good enough to wow a hometown crowd and maybe get him a full ride at a middling college where he would have performed yeoman's work on a capable team, but that LeBron-level fantasy was never destined to happen. The fact that he had killed a sixteen-year-old cheerleader and gotten away with it had little to do with the crash and burn of Donny's hoop dreams.

The Raffins—père and mère—poured a fortune into their golden boy's defense, hiring high-profile attorneys to employ obscure legal techniques, exploit iffy loopholes, and passionately interpret each fact in the light most favorable to Donny's case, while the overworked, underpaid assistant DA dogpaddled frantically to keep his head above water.

For those reasons and the silence of my client, Donald Raffin was found not guilty, and in the twelve years since the crime, no other credible suspect had been put forward.

As Donny set a Smurf-blue cocktail in front of the barfly a couple stools down from me, I signaled for a refill.

The few patrons at that early hour were set with their steins and stems for the moment, freeing Donny to venture into chat-me-up territory while gifting my glass with another fat pour.

"So, how long you in town for?"

"What makes you think I don't live here?" I asked, bringing my eyebrows together in what I hoped was a look of puzzlement.

As he pulled the towel from his shoulder and began polishing a glass from the drying rack, Donny nodded at my phone on the bar. When I'd taken the cell from my pocket, I'd made sure to grab the motel key, one of those throwbacks hanging on a thick ring with a big, plastic rectangle displaying the room number. The display was for a room at a motel that did not exist.

Grinning good-naturedly, I pointed at Donny and said, "Pretty observant guy."

"In this line of work, I have to be," he responded, a self-effacing shrug dismissing the idea that his deduction was anything special.

"Yeah, same in my line."

"And what kind of work do you do?"

With that, the bonding had officially begun, so while Stephie professionally scoured Donny's condo, I wove a tale of spying on cheating wives and tracing deadbeat dads, a low-rent PI story that lasted through two more scotches. I didn't think I could gag down another, so I put a fifty on the bar and extended my right hand.

"I'm Joe, by the way," I volunteered.

"Don," he said, shaking my hand.

"Well, good-night, Don. Maybe I'll see you tomorrow." With that, I eased off the stool, touching down on my left leg and wincing.

"You okay there, Joe?"

"Yeah," I snorted, in response to his pre-paid concern. "Just a little memento from Bush's bogus war. Or, as we grunts on the ground called it: shock and *aw, shit!*"

I ordered a turkey sandwich from room service to sop up the rotgut scotch, and a bottle of spring water to flush it away. I was about to have dessert—two full-strength Bayer's—when Stephie knocked.

"Nothing," she growled, striding past me as I held open the door.

"Balls."

"I looked in places a DEA agent wouldn't think of, so, unless you want me to go back and steam off the wallpaper, I can confidently report it isn't there."

"It" was the blue and gold Hermès scarf Tina Kemp had been wearing as she left her parents' home for the last time, an accessory that was not around her neck when her body was found seventeen hours later, sprawled under a tree on the large, wooded lot whose path provided a shortcut between home and cheerleading practice.

If Stephie hadn't found the scarf in Donny's condo, it wasn't there. She was the most canny, resourceful operative I'd ever hired, vastly overqualified for the job I'd given her after she tanked her law enforcement career. With a criminology degree from USC and an idealistic desire to clean up LA one perp at a time, Stephanie Diaz had joined the police force, but when a superior got handsie, she had to choose among the limited options prior to #MeToo: silence, ineffectual HR, or a knee to the jewels. Stephie took a knee and her future disappeared in a swirly flush.

Though she had desperately needed the job I offered, she clarified her position explicitly in that first interview.

"To be clear, I don't do windows and I don't do the boss."

"My mother will be *so* relieved to know her son's virtue is secure."

Those two statements established our working relationship and, four years later, neither of us has colored outside the lines.

"What now?" she asked.

She had searched Donny's bar the day before and he didn't own any other real estate.

"Tomorrow you check for a bank deposit box or storage unit, anywhere he could have stashed his souvenir. I've got one more night of bromancing, although I'm not sure my liver can take enough of that kerosene Donny calls a well drink to seem convincingly hammered when I lay down a C-note."

"There's a workaround for that," she offered.

The next day, while Stephie did legwork on a possible secret stash location, I briefed my client by phone and set up a meeting with her for the end of the week. By four-thirty I was back at Donny's bar and grateful for Stephie's booze hack.

With anticipation of a generous tip inspiring Donny to pour heavier and heavier, my two fingers of scotch looked more like a whole hand by that third night, but a pair of hotel washcloths, rolled up tightly and stuffed into a Ziploc bag in my jacket pocket, were ready to suck it up.

Our previous conversations had been all about me. Now it was time to draw Donny in, get him comfortable sharing with his new amigo.

"To my first unicorn," I said, hoisting my glass in a salute, then making a sip look like a hefty slug.

Donny chuckled. "Okay, I'll bite."

"Well, D-man, ask any PI and he'll tell you nickel and dimers are the worst thing about our profession. Wifey demands pics of her hubby boning his secretary, but balks at underwriting the gas mileage to follow Casanova to his no-tell mo-tel thirty miles away."

Donny nodded in solemn understanding, probably recalling a skimpy leave-behind after some bachelorette party did six rounds of tequila shots before moving on to a more glamorous watering hole.

"And the guys are just as bad. Every hairy pair thinks he's a frickin' CPA, challenging each line item on my invoice after I've busted my hump digging up enough dirt to bury his old lady and guaran-goddamn-tee he gets custody of those kids he doesn't give a rat's patoot about."

A scribble in the air above a table caught Donny's eye, so he hustled away to close out a tab, while I turned my back on the security camera as if scanning the room for a familiar face, then dumped my drink into my pocket.

By the time Donny returned, two square feet of Egyptian cotton were soaking up the swill so I tapped my glass for another and went on spinning my tale.

"Every morning you get up and pray this is the day someone walks in and hands you a blank check," I continued, as he aimed an arc of blended malt into my glass. "Someone who appreciates your hard work and doesn't question the value you put on it."

"A unicorn."

"Bingo. And I finally scored me one."

I could see Donny reconsidering the disparity between my big-spender tips and Dumpster-dive wardrobe. He must've figured I was on a lavish per diem, but hadn't yet collected the end money.

"The only catch is I gotta seriously upgrade my action for a unicorn. No skulking in the bushes hoping to get a boink shot through the curtains. Gotta go high tech. Gotta use Jedi mind tricks on the client's target."

Wrapping my fingers around the glass and pretending to take a mouthful, I watched Donny nod his head in understanding.

"So, an A-list client requires an A-game strategy," he volunteered.

"Damn straight, my friend."

With the beginning signs of slurring, I told him of the need to distract the target, whether it was an embezzling employee or an ex who'd made off with a few pieces of heirloom jewelry. I deliberately left homicide out of the mix.

"I divert his or her attention away from their own crimes long enough to make my move. I call it setting the pick."

Donny's face brightened at the reference.

"You a B-ball fan?"

"Big time. Always regretted being too short to play," I said, pivoting the convo onto my mark. "You, though, you must be what? Six-four? Six-five?" He was six-three, but as women have known for eons, pretending to see an inch or two more than what's actually there helps get you what you want. "You ever play?"

Now it was my turn as bartender, listening to Donny relive his glory days, asking questions to keep him going whenever he looked like he thought he might be boring me. I used his time away helping other customers to dump more drinks into my pocket.

After hearing lengthy play-by-plays of his most stellar performances, I belched and drunkenly inquired why he hadn't gone on to the pros. Donny went quiet for a long beat.

"Halfway through my last season in high school, I caught a shit break that ended my chances."

"Knee injury?" I asked sympathetically.

Donny paused again before answering.

"Yeah, something like that."

Having planting the seed, I broke the mood by saying I had to use the head. Donny needed a little breathing room so he could relive his crime.

The remainder of the evening I observed a subdued guy going about his work with little enthusiasm, acknowledging me only when I flagged him for a refill. I had obviously hit the nerve I'd been aiming for.

When Donny rang up a ticket at last call for the seven drinks weighing down the right side of my jacket, I didn't even glance at it. Instead, I swayed on my feet alongside the bar stool and handed him a hundred-dollar bill.

"For all us hard-working guys who got screwed over by the world," I drunkenly mumbled, folding his fingers around the Benjamin with a quick, hetero squeeze of solidarity.

There may have been a tear in Dapper Donny's eye as I turned and limped out of the bar.

Back in San Francisco thirty-two hours later, relieved of the hairpiece, prosthetic schnozz and homeless-couture suit, I settled into the buttery leather comfort of a reception area couch five minutes ahead of my appointment time with the company's CEO.

Heather Kemp wasn't the media hound a lot of the young tech billionaires were, but as one of the rare females in that elite club, she commanded an empire while remaining down to earth. It was she who came out to greet me and lead me back to her office, rather than a smartly turned-out executive assistant. I know squat about women's fashion, but her well-fitting jeans and boxy, white shirt probably cost more than the Ermenegildo Zegna two-piece wool suit I had worn despite knowing it would make me stick out among her millennial employees for whom every day is casual Friday. I dress for the job I'm being paid to do, and Heather Kemp was paying me a fortune to prove Donald Raffin had raped and murdered her sister Tina.

When she related her story at our first meeting, I pointed out the unlikelihood of getting justice after so long a time, but Heather only smiled and gestured toward the poster on the wall behind her desk, a bold red rectangle punched by her company's mission statement in strong, sans serif letters: Get Creative.

I wasn't sure what she was asking me to do, but I told her murder-for-hire was not on my menu of services.

"If I'd wanted muscle and a gun, I would have looked much further down the food chain than your agency. This requires brains and finesse, because in the eyes of the law Donny's an innocent man."

"So you want me to prove he did it."

"For starters."

Turning up that scarf would have gone a long way toward connecting Donald Raffin to Tina's murder twelve years ago, especially if usable DNA was still present, but after strangling her with it, he must have eventually come to his senses and ditched his souvenir.

Luckily, that wasn't the only blue and gold Hermès scarf with Tina Kemp's DNA on it.

Heather Kemp was a bona fide genius. While still in college, she had created The Safe Room, revolutionary software to protect computers from viruses embedded in emails. Any incoming that looked dodgy could be moved to The Safe Room before opening, keeping its contents—including malevolent hitchhikers—trapped within impenetrable firewalls. If the comm was clean, a keystroke released it back to the user's list; if not, another stroke burned it to cyber ash.

The sales of The Safe Room for personal computers made her a multi-millionaire before she earned her bachelor's degree, but the follow-up version, Stadium, enabled corporations to routinely run *all* their communications through it in nanoseconds, preventing breaches, hacks and theft of customer data. Few companies risked operating without Stadium, and Heather became one of the richest women in the world.

Successful businesswoman now, but once upon a time she had been a thirteen-year-old jealous of her popular sibling, so when Tina Kemp bought the Hermès scarf in Jackson High's school colors, little sis had to have one, too.

Tina's paychecks from a mall food court smoothie franchise, combined with her babysitting earnings, finally put the designer accessory within her reach.

Heather shoplifted hers.

"My parents would have killed me if they'd found out," she had explained at our earlier meeting. "So I only wore mine on days when Heather *didn't* wear hers, hoping my mother would assume I had borrowed it from Tina."

Although the sisters attended the same school, the three-year age gap put them in different classes on opposite sides of the campus, virtually eliminating the possibility of their crossing paths, but guilt began to gnaw at Heather's conscience. What if security cameras had caught her cramming the scarf up the sleeve of her hoody and the police were tracking her down? What if Mom put two and two together and marched her younger daughter back to the shop to make restitution?

"I was going to hide the thing in a corner of my closet and forget about it, but then I figured a way to rid myself of the tainted scarf and still be able to flaunt the fashion statement around my peers."

She switched her stolen Hermès for Tina's righteously acquired one, a conscience-assuaging swap that could only make sense to a thirteen-year-old. Heather resumed wearing the scarf on days her sister did not.

Then came the afternoon when Tina loosely tied hers around her neck before leaving at three-thirty for two hours of cheer practice.

"I was the only one home, the only one who saw what she was wearing when she walked out the door that last time."

A jogger had found Tina early the following morning, before an official search had even begun, so Heather was never asked by the police what her sister was wearing when she left the house. "My dad identified her body and I assumed he had seen the scarf around her neck. Still scared of being caught out as a shoplifter, I hid mine and never put it on again."

At the trial, which Heather's parents did not allow her to attend, two of Donny's teammates supplied an alibi for him and he explained away his DNA on her clothes by saying they'd had a mutually desired make-out session right after school. Since the police never found the murder weapon, could proffer no believable motive, and were unable to disprove the boy's claim that he and Heather had been keeping their relationship secret from their friends, the DA's case unraveled, and Donny was acquitted.

"Then, at Homecoming my junior year, one of the twelfth-grade girls showed up with Dapper Donny on her arm. Having a college man as a date was a mark of sophistication, and he had become somewhat of a wronged hero since his exoneration in my sister's death two years earlier.

"His grin and swagger were as cocky as they had always been, and, true to his sartorial affectations, he wore an ascot with his blue blazer, instead of a tie."

She switched her stolen Hermès for Tina's righteously acquired one, a conscience-assuaging swap that could only make sense to a thirteen-year-old. Heather resumed wearing the scarf on days her sister did not.

From Stephie's prior recon at Donny's business, I knew he kept a fully-loaded Colt Commander behind the bar, but my carry choice for the occasion needed to be low-rent enough to match my Willy Loman loser charade, so I settled on a Cobra Arms Freedom .380, available everywhere for under two hundred bucks. Purchased virgin-fresh so as not to have a track record with law enforcement, it was destined for the Pacific Ocean after a single use.

Yes, I intended to kill Donald Raffin, but only after I heard him confess, and only in self-defense.

Donny greeted me like an old friend when I showed up two weeks later and parked myself on my previous perch. He set a drink in front of me before I had a chance to ask, and I spent the evening filling my pocket with booze. To his question about my progress, unicorn-wise, I responded with a sly smile.

"Closing in, D. Big payday coming soon."

"Let me know when you make your score and scotch'll be on the house that night."

"Then I'll be sure to get here early and drink till closing time." We both chuckled, two pals sharing a joke.

I left nothing to chance. Stephie disabled the bar's security cameras in the middle of the night, long enough for me to fire two shots from Donny's Colt into a wooden block, but not enough for the security company to register anything more than a quick blip in their system. I retrieved the brass before emptying out the gun and inserting two

Hollywood cop-show bangers into the chamber and top slot of the magazine.

We didn't dick with the exterior camera of the pawn shop across the street, as it was sure to be pulled by the police and would neatly supply an ending to the story they'd reconstruct. The street lights at either end of the alley a block down from the bar were a different thing, however, and Stephie assured me they would not be working at closing time the next night.

Our exit ride was an anonymous heap with a tag too mud-caked to be readable, and was destined to be parked in a local storage unit pre-paid for a year. Stephie would return then and have it towed, sans tag, to a salvage yard.

The only wild card in the mix was the scarf. I had Heather's, but if Donny had burned the original when he finally wised up to the stupidity of holding onto a murder weapon, my ploy might not be effective. I could only hope the shock of seeing it after so many years would confuse him long enough for me to force his hand. And, if he had merely tossed the scarf in a trash can, he'd assume it had somehow been retrieved.

On our last evening in Baltimore, Stephie carefully positioned two sealed packs of prop blood onto my torso, avoiding the heart/lung area that would make the "injuries" look fatal on the security footage after I activated them. She went for a high shoulder shot on the left side, eighteen inches above what would appear to be an entry wound nicking my belt toward one edge of the strapped-on paunch.

If Stephie felt as awkward as I did being alone with her, half-naked in a hotel room, she did a great job of concealing it, but when they make the movie of my life, the actress playing her will pull together the front of the frayed shirt to hide the fakery, then slowly do up the buttons while gazing meaningfully into Bradley Cooper's eyes. In the real-life scene, she slapped the sticky pads one last time to make sure they adhered to my skin and said, "Okay, Fudd. Go get that wascally wabbit."

I didn't show at the bar till after ten, as much swagger in my stride as the bogus limp allowed. Responding to Donny's questioning look, I gave two thumbs up and a big, shit-eating grin. He high-fived me as I slid onto my usual perch.

"Congrats, Joe. You're drinking free tonight."

"In that case, make it a double."

Confident he would see at least a hundred-dollar tip, Donny happily poured for me till last call. As the final patrons staggered out into the night, I said, "Why don't you lock the door and I'll buy *you* a round for a change." I sweetened my slurred invitation by laying down a pair of Benjamins, making sure to touch them only with my fingercotted pointer and thumb. I shook my head to signal I was done when he pointed at my glass, so he gave it a quick wash and set it on the drying rack.

"Did you finally nail your target?" he asked, once he had pulled a draft for himself and settled on the backless, wooden stool behind the bar.

"Let's just say he won't ever duplicate the crime that brought him to my attention."

In his eagerness to hear about my success and earn his own tidy payoff, Donny didn't notice all slurring had vanished from my speech. It would be another several minutes before the registering of that fact would pile onto the mounting realization that he was in way over his head, that I was not even close to being the man he *thought* he was cultivating.

"Come on, Joe, I want details. You're killin' me here," he said with inadvertent prescience.

"Okay, so long time ago, this asshole got away with doing something really horrible, in part because two other assholes alibi'd him to the moon and back."

His eyes were still bright with interest as he raised his pilsner glass and drained off an inch of beer, meaning the penny hadn't dropped yet. That was about to change.

"The thing is, I looked into those alibi A-holes and learned they were just schlubby jocks from barely middle-class homes. And yet, when they went away to junior college and a trade school the following year, each of them was driving a brand-new Corvette."

All the anticipatory excitement drained from Donny's face. He didn't show fear when he carefully set his glass down on the bar, but we had quite a few steps left in our dance.

"Who the fuck *are* you?" he growled.

"I'm your buddy Joe, from Austin," I answered, the big, dopey grin on my face immortalized on the security camera aimed at me. "I'm curious; did you know it was your mom who bought the cars, not your dad? I guess she really wanted to protect her baby boy."

His eyes darted to the front door.

"Oh, don't worry, D. I didn't bring backup."

I could see he was trying to figure out if I was telling the truth, and I respected him for not jumping the gun, so to speak, before making sure. After all, I had lied about everything else up to that point.

"Pretty clever of you to tell the cops you'd had a make-out session with Heather—totally willing on her part—right after final class that afternoon. Explained away all that incriminating DNA of yours *on* the body but not *in* it," I goaded. "But the stroke of near-genius was telling them—and I bet you got all teary-eyed when you told them, right, Donny? When you said you had stopped yourself from going all the way because you had too much respect for her? That way, her mysterious assailant, who thought far enough ahead to pack a condom, couldn't possibly have been the big basketball hero."

Through tightly clenched teeth, he asked, "Do you want money? Is that what this is about?"

"No, but I do want to show you something." He stiffened when I reached into the pocket of the jacket I had draped over the back of the adjacent barstool, but didn't go for his piece. I pulled out a clear plastic bag containing the blue and gold Hermès scarf and placed it on the bar.

"Bet you never thought you'd see *this* again, did you?" He seemed to deflate in the wake of my debunking of his alibi, the description of his means, and the presentation of the murder weapon, but I knew he was playing possum, waiting for the right moment to strike. I allowed the rubber bulb for the blood packs to slide from my sleeve into my left hand.

"Are you here to arrest me?"

"I don't have that kind of juice. Besides, you were exonerated. Double-jep, remember? So, no, I'm not here to arrest you. I'm here to kill you."

He glared, then spat out the words he'd been dying to say for more than a decade, hoping to distract me while he eased his right hand over the edge of the bar above where the Colt rested.

"That little prick-tease led me on for weeks and she deserved everything she got!"

With that, he brought up the gun and fired twice from only a few feet away. I gave two quick squeezes with my left hand, and red stains bloomed at my shoulder and waist.

Making sure to look shocked and terrified, I lurched off the stool, reaching once again into the folds of my jacket while Donny pulled the trigger again and again without further success. His final expression before collapsing behind the bar was one of incomprehension as I unloaded the little Cobra into him.

Grabbing the jacket and holding it against my "wounds" to explain the lack of a blood trail from such grievous injuries, I stepped up onto the bar rail to peek over the edge at Dapper Donny's body, while surreptitiously scooping up the plastic bag.

I knew the homicide cops who viewed the footage would see a dumpy guy checking to see if the man who'd inexplicably opened fire on him was dead, but the action existed only as cover for me to drop the brass I had collected after firing Donny's Colt into that block of wood, a parting gift for the forensics guys.

Clutching the jacket to my side, giving a panicky look around the bar, I staggered to the door and made my exit.

I could not afford to morph prematurely into Keyser Söze, because my escape was being recorded by the security cam across the street, so I maintained the limp all the way to the corner. Turning out of the camera's POV, I slid into the idling junker with Stephie behind the wheel.

# TOMBSTONE DODGE

## Vincent H. O'Neil

I did this particular job because my wife asked me to. I'd do anything for her, no matter how dangerous it might be.

Ninety percent of what I do is fool people. Make them think I'm someone they can trust when I truly don't have their best interests at heart. Fake names and false addresses roll off my tongue like the alphabet, and I have never been found out. When each of these jobs is done, the most important part is that nothing links back to me. To the real me.

With a skill set like that, I was hired as soon as I applied for the temporary position of night security man for the U Lock It Up self-storage company. Harvey, the sixty-year-old I would be replacing for the two weeks of his annual vacation, took me through my duties.

"Got two of these locations." Harvey walked me down a row as he talked. Long, one-story cinderblock buildings were to either side of us, segmented into storage units. Each of them had a metal roll-up door like a car garage, but the whole setup reminded me of those above-the-ground cemeteries you see in so many horror movies. Ranks of stone facades with silent gates, no activity, and limited vision. Downright claustrophobic. "I call this site Tombstone and the other one Dodge. You gotta entertain yourself while you're walking your shift, so I imagine I'm Wyatt Earp, patrolling the streets of the towns I protect."

"Ever have to shoot it out like he did?" I smiled to make it clear I was joking. I liked Harvey as soon as I met him, and knew he'd been doing this job for ten years.

"That would be hard—no guns allowed. All we carry is an emergency radio." He wore a brimmed hat and a light blue uniform with no patches or badges. "Ya see, this is a no-frills operation. No alarm system, no security cameras, and only one guard for two properties. People rent units by the month, pay in cash, and no questions are asked."

"So, what exactly am I supposed to be doing?"

"You are the uniformed presence that prevents break-ins. Period. You walk an hour at each site, all night long. Gate's electric, renters enter and leave using an access badge, and the place is available twenty-four seven."

"Ever any trouble?"

"We're so low-end that no self-respecting thief would hit us. Now, many of our renters are on the ragged edge, so you may encounter some weird stuff from time to time. But as long as they're not breaking into anything, I suggest you pretend you didn't see any of that." He'd stopped, giving me a deep stare from behind his glasses. "But if you do come across a break-in, the advice is almost the same. Pretend you didn't see it, hit the emergency button on the radio, and get outta there. The call goes right to the cops, but in this part of town they don't come fast. Remember you're alone out here."

"You do this all night, every night?"

"Right now, I do. Normally there's a weekend guard, Dave, young man like yourself. Good guard, reliable, been here three years. Someone pushed him off a subway platform, tore up his knee. Normally he walks the entire two weeks I'm gone, but this time it'll be you."

Of course, I already knew about Dave and Harvey and the business's absentee owners. My wife has sources of information all over the city, and one of them belongs to a burglary crew led by a tall redhead nicknamed Rooster Mike. Rooster Mike had been tipped off that one U Lock It Up storage unit contained treasures belonging to our city's biggest organized crime family, the Dantonio's. Rooster Mike allegedly knew which one to hit, and had arranged Dave's injury so that a rookie guard would be on watch when Harvey was gone. My wife's contact in Rooster's crew feared the replacement guard might do something unpredictable, and had asked her to make sure that wouldn't happen.

By getting the job, I'd already accomplished half my assignment. My dear wife's contact didn't know which night the robbery would occur, or even which site—Dodge or Tombstone—contained the target. It really didn't make a difference to me, because the second half of my assignment was even simpler—don't interfere. If everything went smoothly, I wouldn't have to do anything but report a break-in that had occurred while I was patrolling the other site.

Even so, I took the precaution of climbing up two utility poles on the day of my first shift. It's amazing, the things you can get away with in broad daylight if you're wearing a hard hat and a reflector vest. I installed one video camera for each site, controlled by a monitor in my car. I left the view wide, pointed up the rows so I would know when the break-in occurred. Yes, I was supposed to be three miles away when that happened, but you see my wife is a little removed from the action these days. She's forgotten how quickly things go to pieces, and how important it is to have someone you trust who can swear to what actually happened.

And so I walked two entire nights without incident, alternating between Dodge and Tombstone. It was terribly boring, and I began to understand why Harvey told himself stories about Wyatt Earp to pass the time. I tried it myself, but more personal thoughts pushed the Old West lawman away. The setting, silence, and solitude didn't help. Walking through those desolate, identical rows for hours on end let my mind shift to the memories of all the people I'd tricked over the years.

I really shouldn't let it bother me. They weren't innocents—not by a long shot—and all of them had done things to bring my fraudulent presence into their lives. Even so, I'd deceived them into trusting me and they'd paid dearly for it. I was never around when they discovered they'd been had, but I couldn't keep from wondering what that moment of awful realization had been like for each of them. Did they think about me, curse me, or fantasize revenge against me? Did they now measure their lives in two segments, the time before they met me and the long years after I changed their existences?

When these twinges of remorse start to grow, I always think of my wife. We both chose this work, and we're both good at it. It's a risky life we lead, and in my specific role getting found out could mean anything from a beating to a bullet. Sometimes I wonder if it's time to step away from the action, to recognize I've pushed my luck enough and let someone else take these chances. That idea is almost immediately chased away by the shaming thought of telling my wife I wanted to move off the playing field and onto the sidelines. I know she'd understand and even agree, but in some way, I knew I'd feel diminished. I'm a big help to her, and very few people can do this as well as I can.

After two long nights of walking and thinking too much, I was thrilled to see activity on the monitor while driving toward Dodge at 3 AM. Rooster Mike's people were pro's, and they drove a large truck straight down one row in the back of Tombstone. Turns out they'd cut the fence in case anyone was watching the entrance.

I'd barely turned around on the empty streets before they stopped in front of one unit. It took them some time to get the rolling door open, and so I got back just as the five of them started carrying out large watertight drums presumably loaded with money. Pulling the car up at a spot outside the fence that I'd scouted days before, I climbed up a tree and dropped to the ground on the other side.

Moving silently, I reached a corner where I could see the truck, the thieves, and the unit's interior. They'd turned on the lights, and I was just getting intrigued by the large stacks of document containers when things got out of hand.

"You guys ever hear of a silent alarm?" A deep male voice hollered as two figures rushed up to the group. Dark hair and leather jackets. They both had guns, and one had a shoulder bag. I recognized the man without the bag as Tony Blue, a minor leader in the Dantonio family.

"Tony?" Rooster Mike stepped forward while the rest of his crew froze in place. "What are you doing here?"

"Rooster, do you have *any idea* whose stuff this is?" Tony Blue sounded more annoyed than angry.

"This is *yours*?" Rooster looked around. "I swear I didn't know."

"Well that's too bad. For all of you."

"You gonna shoot us all? Right here?"

"We're not shooting anybody." Tony Blue looked at his companion, who was reaching into the bag. "Do it."

The other man pulled out something that looked like an olive drab thermos.

"What's that, Tony?" Rooster asked, already stepping back.

"You idiot. Know what's in those boxes?"

"Hey, we didn't even see those. Right, guys?"

"Not good enough. Because of you, we gotta torch them."

The pieces of the puzzle fell roughly into place. My wife's interest in that storage unit had nothing to do with drums of money. Those document boxes contained important evidence or strong blackmail material. Some of it must have involved the other crime families, for Tony Blue to have standing orders to burn them up if they were compromised.

The bomb guy yanked something off the thermos, and I knew I couldn't let him toss that thing. My wife wanted those boxes and, like I said, I'd do anything for her no matter how dangerous. So I hit the emergency button on the radio, drew the pistol I wasn't supposed to have, pointed it from behind the corner, and yelled the words that I'm never supposed to speak.

"Police! Drop your weapons and get on the ground!"

Shoulder Bag Guy must have just finished arming the device, because he turned and tossed it straight at me. One moment it was flipping end over end through the air, and the next I was flying backward. My eyes filled with orange flame, shorted out with bolts of lightning when I hit my head, and finally resolved into flashing blue lights.

I smelled smoke when I sat up, and had to swat out several embers on my uniform. My ears rang even as I found my pistol and tucked it away, but when my vision cleared the whole scene was overrun with cops. Tony, his buddy, and the entire Rooster crew were facedown and handcuffed. A male detective in plainclothes and body armor jogged up to me.

"You okay, Steve? You look a little overcooked."

"I'm fine, Marty. Where's my wife?"

"I'll get her." He walked off toward the lockup. "Hey Lieutenant, that guard wants to speak with you."

A tall woman in a long coat came outside. She stopped to give orders to the officers loading the prisoners, and then walked over. She stood over me with her hands on her hips.

"Why are you here? Didn't I tell you to just do your rounds?"

"They would have burned up all those boxes if it wasn't for me." I felt for my eyebrows and didn't find them. "That's what this was really about, right?"

She knelt, and whispered in my ear. "We been trying to find this stash for years. There's enough dirt in there to put half the city behind bars. Good job."

"You needed Rooster to show you which one it was."

"Yep."

The ringing in my ears lessened a bit. "And Rooster found out from Dave, the guard with the busted knee."

"Just how would you know that?" she asked.

"The regular guy, Harvey, is too dedicated."

"Well you're right. Good old Dave saw some Dantonio muscle at this locker one night and figured it would be a good score. He tipped off Rooster, and my snitch in his crew tipped me off. We still didn't know which unit it was, or I never would have involved you." She wiped soot off my cheek and stood up. "You know, that Dave character had them push him off that platform so he'd be in the clear. He figured the Dantonio's would blame the rookie guard. You."

"Well thank goodness I'm not me, most of the time."

"You undercovers." She blew me a kiss before walking off. "You're all crazy as hell." 🔫

# STAR WITNESS

## Joe Giordano

Madeline called. The much younger wife of my first precinct captain. She's a redhead who dolls-up like a Vogue model. When I worked for her husband, she'd send me on errands. After I'd delivered dry cleaning or their white poodle Fifi from the groomer, she'd touch me enough to make me uncomfortable. Cancer took the captain, and I hadn't heard from her in years. Her call requesting my help had the familiar tone I remembered of expecting me to comply. My loyalty to her late husband got me to respond. My name's Bragg, and I'm a homicide gold-shield detective out of Brooklyn South.

She answered the door in a clinging purple sequined sheath dress and looked me up and down. "Blue eyes, you've kept yourself in shape."

She never used my name. With a tinge of annoyance, I asked, "What's up?"

She pointed to a brown cardboard package about the size of a shoebox lying face down on her porch. "I can't see the label," she said. "I'm afraid it's a bomb."

Not since the 1950s Mad Bomber scare had Brooklyn residents been as tense. In the prior fifteen days, five IEDs had exploded in various Brooklyn neighborhoods killing six people. The newspapers screamed for results, but we rope-a-doped their questions because there was no progress in the case to report. We cautioned the public against opening suspicious packages, which is why I received Madeline's call.

"Did you order anything from Amazon?" I asked.

"I'm expecting shoes from Saks tomorrow."

I turned over the box. The label had her name and address. My penknife sliced through the packaging, finding red, nearly-nude, ankle-strap sandals inside.

She put a hand on my waist. "Come in. I'll get you something to drink while I try them on."

"I have an appointment with my boss," I said quickly.

As I turned to leave, her face looked sulky.

Lieutenant Dixon was a grizzled African American. He waved me into his office. Before my butt hit the chair, he said, "I'm assigning you a partner."

I stiffened. "I work best alone."

"We're going to test that theory."

"Tell me," I said stifling my annoyance.

Dixon shoved a manila folder across his desk.

"Casey London," I said, my eyebrows rising. "A woman?"

Dixon responded sarcastically. "Nice to know you can read."

I flipped a page. "She made detective five years younger than I did."

"She's probably smarter than you."

I almost made a snarky remark about affirmative action. Dixon was a decent boss and a good cop, but he might've taken it personally. "She's hardly out of diapers," I said.

He gave me a mirthless smile. "Jealous?"

I stammered. "Not at all."

"I expect you'll want to coach her."

"Oh, she'd love that," I said smirking.

"The photo doesn't do her justice."

Casey London's head shot pictured her eight-point police hat pulled down shading her eyes. A take-me-seriously glare into the camera couldn't hide that she was gorgeous.

I didn't want a partner, certainly not one who had something to prove and inexperienced to boot. I made a final attempt to dissuade him. "Why don't you pair her with somebody else?"

Dixon raised a finger. "Make this work or your next partner will have halitosis that will curl your toenails."

Unambiguously clear. "Where is she?"

Dixon pointed toward the squad room. "I'm assigning the two of you to work with the FBI on this bomber case," he said. "We've hit a wall, and they want us to re-interview the victims' families. Pick up London and get started. When you're done, report to Agent Gerald Blander at Federal Plaza in Manhattan."

I recognized London from the photo. Her ebony black hair was tied in a ponytail and she'd put on just a trace of lipstick and makeup. She wore a gray pinstripe pantsuit with a white blouse. She stood from behind her desk, and I took the hand she offered.

"Bragg," I said. "Pleased to be working with you."

"Do you have a first name?"

"Just Bragg."

"That's what I heard." She said in a mock-gruff voice, "I'm Bragg and I work alone." She chuckled.

Terrific. She greets me with a zinger. "Don't believe everything you hear," I said.

"Lieutenant Dixon said you were the best detective in the squad."

Followed by a compliment. "I take that back."

She pulled keys from her pocket. "I requisitioned a car."

"I'll drive," I said.

"We've met for two minutes and you're already pulling the male thing?"

Oh boy, it's going to be like that. She didn't wait for my protest before she led me out of the precinct.

Riding shotgun in the car, I punched an address into the GPS. "Let's start with victim number one, Rufus Jones." As she drove toward the Bedford Stuyvesant Brooklyn neighborhood, I asked, "Why did you become a cop?"

"My father retired on the job, and I was an only child. He attended my academy graduation before passing. Heart attack."

She has blue in her blood. Good. "My sympathies," I said.

She nodded.

"You get a lot of the 'male thing?' " I asked matter-of-factly.

She gave me a brief sidelong glance I interpreted as her deciding how to take my question. "They come in three sizes, dictatorial, fatherly, and lecherous, sometimes in combination," she said. "By the way, did Lieutenant Dixon tell you to coach me?"

"I figured you'd enjoy that like kidney stones."

She had a hearty laugh. The smile transformed her face. Stunning.

At my stare, she asked, "What?"

"You have spinach in your teeth."

She started to reach for the rear-view mirror to look, then stopped herself. "I didn't eat spinach."

"My mistake." My eyes were back on the street. I spotted a ten-year-old girl taking a selfie with an iPhone. Murder, I thought, the ultimate narcissistic act.

We arrived at a modest asphalt shingle home and Rufus Jones's wife received us. Stepping inside, we saw that yellow crime scene tape was strung across the stairs that led to a basement. We declined her offer of coffee and sat at a wooden kitchen table. The woman was around thirty-five, but grief had aged her. We both expressed sympathy for her loss.

"The FBI practically accused Rufus of killing himself assembling a bomb," Mrs. Jones said, obviously upset. "Only after the next explosion, did they classify his death as a homicide."

The woman had a right to be pissed. Still, I had a job to do. "I'm sure you've been asked this question before, but did anyone wish Rufus harm?"

Mrs. Jones teared up. "He was polite to everyone."

We reiterated our sympathies before we left for Brownsville, the second victim's home, eighteen-year-old Lionel Green.

His parents were indignant. "The FBI thought he'd been attacked because of a drug dispute," his father said, his voice rising. "Lionel never got involved in gangs."

Mrs. Green's face was sad when she said, "We knew Rufus Jones from our Atlantic Avenue Social Club. We told the FBI this might be a racially motivated hate crime, targeting African Americans."

The poor woman was grieving, so I just listened to her theory and didn't mention that the next victims were a Hispanic grandmother, two Italians, and a Jew.

The third victim, Juanita Alvarez was eighty and living alone in Bushwick. The IED detonated when she picked up the package at her front door. We drove past the crime scene. There was no one to speak to, so no point in stopping.

A tripwire on a jogging path in Prospect Park set off the fourth explosion killing Bill and Sarah Esposito. The bomber had evolved to use a more sophisticated device and triggering mechanism, an unsettling thought. The Espositos were a professional couple without known enemies, another dead end.

The fifth bomb, like the others, was filled with carpenter nail shrapnel and TATP, a volatile crystalline powder made from acetone and hydrogen peroxide, constituents of nail polish remover and hair bleach. The IED killed Meir Abraham, sixty, an Orthodox Jew at his Midwood home. Nobody we spoke to could imagine anyone wanting him dead.

Because the materials used in the bombs were commercially available, the FBI had inquired at Home Depot and other retail outlets about large purchases of the bomb's components but without success.

Sitting together in the car, Casey asked, "What connects these people?"

I shrugged. "The killer travels freely. Nobody reports his movements as suspicious. A postal worker? Perhaps he works for UPS or FedEx, so his deliveries seem natural?"

She expanded on my speculation. "Could be an Uber driver. While he's picking up a fare, he drops off a bomb?"

Over the radio, we heard Lieutenant Dixon's voice. "Head over to FBI headquarters. There's been a break in the case."

Inside Federal Plaza in Manhattan, Agent Gerald Blander, sporting a goatee that gave him the look of a satyr, stood at a podium at the opposite end of a lacquered wooden table large enough to have deforested the Grand Tetons. Like a gauntlet, agents sat along both sides in dull-gray padded chairs. When Casey and I stepped into the room, she stopped conversations. We moved toward the standing overflow in the back. An agent jumped up from his chair and held it for her to sit, which she reluctantly accepted. When he placed his hands on her shoulders, she gently removed them while flashing me a knowing look.

Blander introduced us to the agents in the room before he lit a PowerPoint visual on a large screen saying, "We've received a communication from the murderer."

The room buzzed at the news and my eyes focused on the message, composed of individual small and capital cut out letters. This is Jellyfish speaking. The stupid police and FBI flail away as I lay waste to your safe spaces. Have the newspapers print this letter or reap the consequences.

Jellyfish? This guy really is nuts, I thought.

Blander silenced the room before continuing. "We know the communication came from the killer because he enclosed a piece of the robe Juanita Alverez wore when she was murdered."

The bastard watched her blow to pieces, I thought.

"My assistant is passing out photocopies," Blander said. "Forensics has been scouring the paper for clues including the magazines clipped to create the text. The killer could've worn a cleanroom suit for all the trace evidence we've found. Our profiling people say he's a pissed-off loner. Describes about half of Brooklyn."

An agent piped up. "Do you see any significance in calling himself Jellyfish?"

"Jellyfish have multiple stinging tentacles," Blander responded. "Some species can kill humans."

The room started to buzz again, and Blander regained attention. "Study this document. If you come up with anything, contact me immediately. I'll update you when there's something more to report." He shut down his computer.

Casey and I returned to the precinct and briefed Lieutenant Dixon on the Fed meeting before we headed home. Her parting words were, "I've got some research to do."

Something I didn't see caught her attention.

I gave her my mobile number. "If you come up with anything, call me."

Around two in the morning my phone buzzed me awake.

At my groggy hello, Casey said, "I shouldn't have called."

I yawned. "Too late. What's up?"

"Can you come over to my apartment?"

Oh. Shit. "You can't tell me over the phone?"

Her voice turned cold. "Never mind. I knew this was a mistake."

I let out a long, resigned breath. "Text me your address."

Casey's studio apartment was on the third floor with no elevator. She opened the door wearing jeans and a red pullover and was barefoot. She padded to a brown sofa-sleeper. "I made coffee," she said.

"Good move." I poured a mug. Black.

She sat cross-legged on the couch amid piles of papers and books. I took the tan armchair beside her.

"Jellyfish are members of the subphylum Medusozoa," she said.

I rubbed my eyes. "Better to use short words this early in the morning."

"You've heard of Medusa?"

I humored her. "Snakes for hair and turned men to stone."

"Do you remember who killed Medusa?"

"If we're playing twenty questions, I'll probably nod off."

"Perseus slayed her."

I sipped my coffee. "Okay."

She opened a thick volume and pointed at an entry. "The name Perseus is derived from the Greek verb perthein, to lay waste."

I had no clue where she was going. "Bad dude."

She shuffled papers retrieving the photocopy of the killer's message. She quoted. "'I lay waste to your safe spaces.'"

I kneaded my chin at the flicker of light that appeared in my sleepy brain. "Like perthein. Tenuous but okay. Let's say the killer thinks he's Perseus. How does that help us find him?"

She smiled. "We look to the stars."

"Really?" I asked in a sarcastic tone. "You're pulling out a Ouija Board next?"

She leaned forward. "Look at this." She spread a map of Brooklyn on a glass cocktail table. She'd marked the five bombing locations with red dots.

I leaned closer to see. She smelled like a ripe peach.

"The scatter looks random," I said.

"Did you know that Perseus has his own constellation?" she asked impishly.

I tilted my head. "I'll admit that fact eluded me."

She held up a sheet of transparent film where she'd traced a series of short lines connecting twelve black dots. "I've drawn the main stars of the Perseus Constellation in proportion to the map of Brooklyn." Her smile broadened. "Watch."

She placed the constellation transparency over the map. Five of the twelve black dots covered the five red dots representing murder sites.

"Holy shit," I said.

"See why I asked you here?"

I sat back. "Wait a second. The killer calls himself 'Jellyfish,' so you come up with Medusa who was slayed by Perseus. He writes that he wants to 'lay waste' and you find that Perseus's name derives from a similar Greek verb. You plot a seemingly random set of murders on a Brooklyn map and find a way to overlay five of the stars in the Constellation Perseus to match the five bombing sites."

She was nodding as I summarized her research.

"Are you trying to tell me that we can predict where the killer will strike next by staking out the remaining stars in the constellation?" I asked in a tone of disbelief.

Casey's shoulders sagged a bit. "When you put it that way, it does seem a little farfetched."

"Farfetched? You cobble together a series of connections that maybe only an Ivory Tower Classics Professor could come up with."

She began to gather her notes from the couch.

"Stop," I said. "For nearly three weeks, the entire FBI and Brooklyn PD have been desperate, at a complete loss." I looked at her in admiration. "This is the most brilliant deductive detective work I've seen in my career."

She brightened like a kid lauded for the correct answer in class.

"You need to tell Blander and Dixon what you found," I said.

She stiffened, looking doubtful. "You want me to stand in front of fifty agents and expose my theory to ridicule? What if it all turns out to be a coincidence? I'll be nicknamed 'Medusa.' Cops will snicker when I pass. My career will be over."

I nodded thoughtfully. "I see your point. What do you propose?"

"We'll stake out one of the star locations not yet attacked by the bomber."

My eyebrows rose. "Which one?"

She looked at the map and frowned. "Good question."

"Look," I said, "nobody working on this case has anything better to do but pursue your idea. We need to watch all the neighborhood locations indicated by the seven remaining constellation stars starting first thing tomorrow."

"You and I can't be everywhere at once."

I nodded. "I'll call in favors from the squad. I'll tell the detectives that we have an educated guess where the bomber will strike next."

"You'd spend your credibility for me?" she asked sounding a bit surprised.

"Which star should you and I pick?" I asked.

She placed her finger on 'Algol.' "The ancients termed it the 'Demon Star,' " she said.

By eight the next morning, I'd received commitments from the other Brooklyn South detectives to patrol the locations corresponding to the remaining Perseus Constellation stars. I asked everyone not to tell Lieutenant Dixon what we were doing.

Before we set out, Casey said, "If this fails, the fallout can't only be on your shoulders. We're in this together."

We'd become a team, I thought.

Casey drove her white Smart Car, a vehicle no criminal would suspect of carrying two Brooklyn detectives. We spent the first few hours cruising before we parked in the East Flatbush area where the star Algol pointed us.

Late morning, my phone buzzed: Lieutenant Dixon. I let his call go to voicemail. His message asked where the hell was I and almost every member of his command? His tone indicated that he suspected my hand in everyone's absence. I was in deep shit, and my angst rose contemplating what his dressing down of me would feel like.

After hearing Dixon's voicemail, Casey asked, "What if the bomber takes days to plant his next device? How long can we keep the operation secret?"

I sighed without answering, putting the question out of my mind.

Dixon phoned almost every hour. His final voicemail said that Blander at the FBI insisted on a briefing from me and if I didn't show up at Federal Plaza, I'd better either have the excuse of the century or I'd be walking a beat in the remotest part of Staten Island. As none of the other detectives were answering his calls, he added that he didn't appreciate my organizing a mutiny.

I'd not played his last messages for Casey, but she read my face. "He's angry?" she asked.

"Volcanic," I said, as my stomach churned.

Around four in the afternoon, a blue flower delivery van slowly passed our car. We scrunched down in our seats as we'd done when any vehicle approached. Within ten minutes, the same truck drove by again.

"Lost?" I asked in a doubtful tone.

The third time the van appeared in our rear-view mirror, the driver, with short dark hair in jeans and a brown sweatshirt, stopped and retrieved from the rear a flower arrangement inside a glass vase. He also carefully grabbed a cardboard box. He looked around before he strode to a house, and placed the box on the front step, then reversed course still carrying the flowers.

Casey and I jumped from the Smart Car, shouting 'police' as we drew our Glocks. I held my badge high in the other hand.

The driver was still on the sidewalk, thirty feet from his vehicle. He hesitated and seemed to be deciding if he should run.

"Freeze," I shouted pointing my pistol.

He dropped the vase, splattering glass on the concrete, then ran to the house and retrieved the package.

"Don't move." I steadied my aim, my forefinger covering the trigger.

The subsequent explosion threw Casey and me to the ground. I might've blacked out for a second. My first thought was to feel around to see if I'd been hit with shrapnel. Fortunately, the bomber's body absorbed most of the explosion.

Casey lay next to me with her eyes closed. I crawled over and cradled her in my arms.

One of her eyes opened. "Only if you're Prince Charming, can you kiss me," she said.

She was okay, and I smiled. "Does that make you a princess?"

She grimaced. "My head hurts. Don't make me laugh."

"You were right. The bastard won't hurt anyone else."

The blast must've triggered 911 calls, because we heard sirens approach from a distance.

Casey wriggled out of my arms. "No way I'm allowing anyone to see you holding me."

We were soon approached by vehicles with flashing lightbars coming to a screeching halt. An ambulance took us to Brookdale Hospital for observation.

Lying in the hospital bed, I opened my eyes to see Lieutenant Dixon looking at me rather sternly. "Last time you go off on your own escapade, or we part company," he said.

I nodded.

He took my hand. "Great work, Detective."

The next day, the doctors released us. We stopped at Casey's apartment to gather her notes and headed for the precinct. Agent Gerald Blander sat in Dixon's office. He rose as we entered and said to me, "Congratulations getting that bastard. How did you know where he'd strike next?"

I gestured toward my partner. "It was one hundred percent Casey. She'll give you the rundown."

Blander and Dixon's eyes turned toward her. She explained the Medusa connection, Perseus, the Brooklyn map, and showed them the constellation transparency overlay.

When she'd finished, Blander said, "Impressive. If you ever want a job in the FBI, call me." She smiled as he shook her hand. He nodded a goodbye to Dixon and left without shaking mine.

"I'm calling the Commissioner. You two deserve the Medal for Valor," Dixon said.

She glowed at the prospect. "Thank you, sir."

"Just Casey," I said. "I went along for the ride."

She protested. "We were a team."

Dixon leaned back in his desk chair, inserting his thumbs under his belt. "High profile cases make a career." He gazed at me with a wry smile. "Bragg, one day soon, we'll all be working for her."

At the end of our shift, we headed for the Dead Rabbit, an Irish pub within walking distance.

We sat in a booth. I ordered a Fat Tire Ale, Casey ordered a Jameson 18 Years, neat. She told the blonde waitress to start a tab. She said to me, "We're not having the 'male thing' try to pay for my scotch."

I'd learned not to argue.

We clinked a toast to the end of the case. Sipping the Jameson, she said, "I know what you're thinking."

"Do you?"

"You didn't react to what Dixon said."

"You mean that one day you'll be my boss? He's probably right."

"I won't sleep with my partner," she said.

I was surprised but didn't respond. She was a good detective.

She continued. "If I were your boss, any approach to a subordinate would be considered de facto sexual harassment according to NYPD policy."

"I was never big on Latin words," I said, trying to sound casual.

"Once I'm promoted and no longer your partner but haven't yet assumed the supervisory role, your baby blue eyes might get lucky," she said, with her eyes sparkling.

"Clever," I said masking my pleasure. "Now, you've got me rooting for your promotion."

Casey displayed a self-satisfied smile. "See, I knew what you were thinking."

I'd been outed. "Since you're buying, I'm switching to scotch." I waved the server over and ordered a Jameson.

"Finally," she said in her mock-gruff voice, "you're having a manly drink."

By the end of our evening in the Dead Rabbit, I was well oiled. We both ordered Ubers, hers arrived first and we said goodnight.

I headed for Madeline's house.

She answered the door wearing a pink flannel house coat. Her cheeks and forehead were shiny from whatever night cream she'd applied.

Madeline covered her face. "I look like shit."

Three steps inside the door, we were entwined on the floor. At three in the morning, I awoke in bed beside her, groaning with a headache from Hades. The room was dark, but I didn't want to look at Madeline anyway. I tapped an order for an Uber into my phone as I slipped out of her house, dreading the next time she'd call me.

# WIPEOUT

## Adam Meyer

The inspection was going even better than Dominic had hoped. The guy they'd sent looked a little younger than Dominic himself, maybe mid-twenties, fresh-faced and blond, a corn-fed Midwestern-type so pale it was like he'd never stepped foot on the sand that gave Rockaway Beach its name. He had no clipboard, just an iPad, which he snapped pictures with as he moved this way and that around the basement. His name was Timothy Anderson but he said most people just called him "Tim."

Tim crouched against the floor, his hair flopping down into his face. "Bathroom was here, right?"

"I, ah …" Ma was flapped, just the way she'd been in the days after the storm.

"That's right," Dominic said.

Tim took a shot of what was left of the broken toilet, the porcelain now yellow and green, and made a note in his iPad.

Dominic looked around. It was fourteen months since Hurricane Norma had swept in off the Atlantic and flooded the basement. If he closed his eyes, he could still see it, brownish water seeping in from beneath the window frames and around the back door.

"You really got wiped out," Tim said, snapping another picture. Of what, Dominic had no idea. The whole place had been reduced to empty gray walls and stray bits of loose insulation. Wherever you stood it looked pretty much the same. "You really think you're going to rebuild down here?"

"I hope so," Ma said, glancing at Dominic. "We're just not sure …"

"What she means is, it depends," Dominic said. "On how much money you guys are willing to fork over."

Tim laughed like Dominic had just cracked a good one. But it was no joke. Ma had already spent most of her savings cleaning up the mess: pumping out seawater, knocking down soggy sheetrock, and ripping up moldy carpet. They didn't have flood insurance and the homeowners' policy was a joke. This Rebuild Rockaway program was their last hope to get some money to cover their losses.

"We'll do everything we can to help," Tim said, looking around. "That's a promise."

After a few more minutes of showing Tim around, Dominic led the way up to the kitchen. Tim slid his iPad into a shoulder bag, smiling. "You seem like a good candidate for the program. If you're lucky, you should get enough money to replace the drywall, buy a new washer-dryer, maybe put up some fresh paint."

Dominic felt his whole body tense. "What about my stuff?"

Did he really need to remind this guy of all of the things he'd lost down there? He'd already listed them on the application: a fifty-inch television, his Sony Playstation and two dozen games, a thousand dollars worth of clothes. Not to mention all the comic books and DVDs and the Memory Foam mattress with two sets of silk sheets.

Tim frowned. "It's not my call, it's my supervisor's. But we only reimburse for what's necessary to make your home habitable, including basic appliances. Non-essential elements like carpeting and—"

"You don't even pay for goddamn carpeting? I thought you people were gonna help us."

"I went over this with your mother on the phone." Tim glanced at Ma, then back at Dominic. "Our grants are only meant to cover essential materials and major appliances. If you'd had a kitchen down there, for example, you'd get a lot more money. Or if your heating system had been installed more recently."

So that was why he'd asked about when they'd put in the furnace. Dominic knew they should've been more vague, but Ma was right in there, telling the guy it was twenty-five years old.

"So what're we looking at?" Dominic asked. "How much money we gonna get?"

"We'd have to run a full accounting of—"

"How goddamn much?"

"Sir, these grants aren't meant to replace all that you've lost. The goal is to give folks just enough to start over and then hopefully you can do the rest for yourself." Tim adjusted his shoulder bag, looking away. "If I had to guess I'd say maybe fifteen hundred dollars. Two thousand tops."

"That's a fucking joke."

"I'm sorry you feel that way but I sincerely hope—"

"Get out."

Tim looked at Dominic, blinking. Clearly, he wasn't used to being talked to like this.

"Okay, well, thank you for your time. Someone from our office will be in touch."

Heading out the front door, Tim held the strap of his shoulder bag like an old lady on a crowded subway car. As soon as the storm door swung shut behind him, Dominic turned on his mother. "You knew all this and you let me think they were gonna help?"

"I told you not to get your hopes up." Ma looked sharply at him. "Didn't I?"

"Oh, now it's my fault they're running some kind of shit program?"

His mother pressed her hand to her temple as if she felt a migraine coming on. "I can't talk about this now."

"When are we gonna talk about it then? Huh?" He smacked the wall, hard enough to hurt his hand. "Goddamn good for nothing, all of you'se!"

But he was shouting at himself. His mother was already walking away.

Three days later, Dominic was charging down the Rockaway boardwalk, the wind whipping off the ocean flinging his hair all around. He'd been in a foul mood ever since that inspector came by. He'd hoped a couple beers at Mulligan's would take the edge off but the other guys were getting on his nerves so he left. Now he was making his way down the boardwalk, his head pounding from the too-strong September sun. He plopped down on a bench to rest. A bunch of teenagers kicked around at the edge of the surf. Dominic wished he was one of those dumb kids, no idea how hard life could be, and lit a cigarette.

"You got another one?"

He looked over at the girl who'd asked. Good sized-rack, face as flat as the back end of a shovel, but something in the eyes. Like she was watching you.

"You're Dominic, right?"

He looked at her dumbly, lit a cigarette for her.

"I'm Katherine Geffen. I was a year behind you in school." Deep inhale of smoke. "Most people call me Kat."

Katherine Geffen? No bells were ringing. Hold on … Kat Geffen. *Fat* Kat Geffen. She'd lost a few pounds since high school. Not that she was thin, but the padding around her hips was nothing like the rolls of fat he remembered. She actually looked kind of sexy in her black knee-high skirt and tight-fitting T-shirt.

"How you doing?" he asked.

"Okay. Just heading to work. I wait tables at the Reef." She nodded at an open-front restaurant on the far side of the boardwalk, the kind of place outsiders came to for that beachy feeling. Dominic himself had never been.

"Good for you," he said, thinking it must be nice to have a place to go. Even Fat Kat Geffen had that, and what did he have? No job and no prospects. For a few years after he dropped out of Queens College at least he'd had his own space in the basement, and now he didn't even have that, he was just stuck in his old bedroom, waiting, and for what he had no idea.

He dragged on his cigarette. She did the same, watching him.

"You seem down," she said.

"Yeah, well, our basement got wiped out during Norma and we ain't been able to fix it up yet. My Ma and I were hoping to get a bunch of money from this Rebuild Rockaway program, but now it looks like we won't get shit. If you'll pardon my French."

"Sorry."

"It's all right. Maybe I'll fix things up down there myself, save some money."

Did she remember that he'd nearly failed shop class? That was ten years ago, he doubted it.

"I feel bad for you and your mom."

"Yeah, don't worry. Things'll turn around."

"By the way ..." Kat looked up at the surf, her brown eyes lighting up. "... I know someone who works over there at Rebuild Rockaway. My boyfriend. Andy."

Boyfriend? Fat Kat *had* moved up in the world. Then again, Dominic wasn't surprised. She really did look sexy.

"Your boyfriend, he's an inspector?"

"No, Andy's a supervisor. He reviews the applications and stuff, decides who gets money and how much. I don't know if he could help you out but maybe. I'll tell him about you, say we're old friends."

Friends? Not exactly. He tried to remember if he had ever done anything to her in high school. No, he surely hadn't. Fat Kat was a girl, not a boy, and too far down on the pecking order for him to bother with.

"Thanks," he said. "Can't hurt."

Dominic brooded, thinking about everything he'd lost in the flood: not just the DVDs and the Playstation games and the Bose speakers, but his basic sense of dignity, of feeling like he was a person who mattered. He plucked the cigarette out of his mouth, held it until it burned his fingers. Fat Kat was watching him, her gaze curious and clear.

"Something wrong?" she asked.

"I was thinking. Your boyfriend, if he's pulling the purse strings over there ... maybe he could find a way to get us some extra money."

"Extra? You mean … oh, I don't know about that."

"You could at least talk to him, right? They got these guidelines, see, about how much they can give. I bet if he could adjust our application, make it look like we had a kitchen in the basement, a new heater, he could get us … oh, at least another twenty grand. Whatever he gets, we'd split it down the middle."

"You're talking about lying for the money." She let the cigarette drop between her nicely-tanned legs, sparks flicking across the boardwalk. "I just don't know."

"It's not a lie, we lost twenty grand worth of stuff, easy. And if he's some kind of bigshot over there, then I bet he could figure out how to work the system."

Fat Kat looked out at the ocean, shaking her head. "Seems risky."

"It's too risky, all he has to do is say no. Just ask him, all right?"

Dominic looked out at the place where the ocean and the sky blurred so that you couldn't tell one from the other, then turned back to Kat. She nodded.

"Sure, I'll ask him," she said. "Meet me at the Reef around ten tonight and I'll let you know what he says."

At around nine-thirty, Dominic slipped out of his childhood bedroom and made his way across the faded blue shag in the hall. He was almost to the front door when he heard his mother's voice, sharp as a lobster's claws.

"Dom? You going somewhere?"

"Out."

She moved toward him, her bright red curls silver at the roots. "You know, I been thinking. About that inspector."

"Yeah, I been thinking too. About how I'd like to shove his goddamn iPad where the sun don't shine."

"Dominic, please." She let out a deep breath as if she'd been holding it a long time. "What I thought was, maybe he's right."

"Right about what?"

"Like he said, it's important to help people to take a first step, but then they gotta do the rest for themselves. You know what I'm saying?"

"Not really."

"Dom, I been taking care of you for a long time now, and that's all right, but you need to take care of yourself, too. I mean, you can live here as long as you want, but I can't keep paying for you to hang out at Mulligan's with your buddies all day. Starting next month … you gotta pay your own bills. And you're gonna have to pay rent, too."

She started to turn away, as if she was finished, but he grabbed her arm. "What're you talking about?"

"Just five hundred bucks. That's not much …"

"You're gonna charge me five hundred bucks to live in this shithole? In my own goddamn bedroom?"

Her lower lip started to quiver but her eyes held firm. "It's my house, you know."

"So where am I gonna get all this money? Rent, bills, whatever—you think I can just snap my fingers and get a job?"

"I hear they're hiring down at Rosati's, for parking cars or something."

Dominic shook his head slowly. He was going to take people's keys and smile like a dummy for crumpled dollar bills? Fat chance.

"Or you could talk to Carmelo about getting your old job back."

The only thing more unlikely than him parking cars was working for Carmelo again. After Norma, all the businesses along 116th Street were closed for repairs. A month later, he saw the grand reopening sign at Surfside Pizza, spotted the other guys behind the counter, even that dumb mick who folded the pizza boxes. He went in, Carmelo said that times were tough and they had to go with a leaner crew, blah blah blah. Of course Dominic could've made a stink, but that wasn't his way.

"You want me to pay my own way, fine. I'll get some money and get myself the hell out of this shithole."

He slammed the front door on the way out and left Ma there, alone.

Unbelievable. Three days ago, he'd thought everything was about to turn around, and now his life was shittier than ever. He marched down the sidewalk, hearing the slap of his sneakers and the thrum of his blood in his ears, and headed off to meet Fat Kat Griffin.

The bar at the Reef was filled with Brooklyn hipsters, most of them still wearing their designer shades long after dark. Dominic felt self-conscious just being under the same fake-thatched roof with them, but then he saw Fat Kat struggling to fit herself and a tray full of empties through a gaggle of lamppost-thin girls. Turning, she caught his eye and then looked away again.

He took a table in the corner so he could get a little space from the hipsters and watch Fat Kat work. She had a herky-jerky style, twisting this way and that, always bumping customers and almost spilling stuff. In some ways she was still the girl who got picked last for every team in gym class, yet there was something likeable about her that he'd never noticed. The big smile she got when she served someone. The way she never let any of her stumbles slow her down. Dominic admired that.

After about ten minutes, she wandered over and smiled at him. He looked up at her over the menu and realized he didn't like thinking of her as Fat Kat anymore. The name just didn't suit her these days.

"What can I get you, sir?" Kat asked.

Dominic frowned, wondering what kind of game this was. After that showdown with his Ma he didn't have the patience for any more bullshit.

"So did you talk to your boyfriend about—"

She shook her head, just the slightest bit. "Are you ready to order, sir?"

He looked over as another waitress went by, balancing plates. Okay, Dominic got it. Kat didn't want anyone else to hear, was going to act like she didn't even know him. Dominic didn't mind. He got kind of a thrill out of it.

"Uh, gimme a Bud and a cheeseburger."

"Sure, you got it."

She went off and he sat there, watching some college girls flirt with the hipsters. They wore stretch jeans and tank tops, shivering as the early fall wind swept in off the beach.

When Kat brought his food, she looked at him with a fake smile.

"Get you anything else?"

"Ketchup, I guess."

She brought a plastic bottle and slapped the check on the table. "Here you go, sir."

"Wait, can't we at least talk ..."

She was gone before he could finish. Clearly her boyfriend must've decided not to take Dominic up on his offer. Had he gone a step further than that and reported him to the police? But for what, exactly? Dominic hadn't committed any crime. All he'd done was ask a simple question.

He picked up the check, feeling his stomach clench. He'd charge this to his credit card, but after that talk with Ma, he had no idea where he'd get the money to pay the monthly bill. Then he turned the slip of paper over to check the damage and saw something written in Kat's handwritten scrawl.

MEET ME AT THE OLD PIER AT 11.

He looked across the restaurant at Kat again. She had her back to him and he watched her butt move in the same short black skirt all the waitresses here wore. It looked better on her than most of them, he decided, as he took another sip of his beer.

Ninety minutes later, he sat on the beach by the old pier, which was really just a broken-down row of pilings. Sometimes guys climbed out on the rotting wooden stumps on a dare, trying to see if they could make it out to the end and back. Dominic had done it himself, though not in many years. Probably not since high school, though he couldn't remember for sure. Some of those nights out with his friends had gotten lost in a haze of booze.

"Hey," Kat said, calling out from behind him.

He turned. She was a dark silhouette against the white sand, her skirt kicking up a little in the breeze. He patted the place beside him and she sat. She smelled of fried flounder and spilled beer and something else too, powdery and sweet.

"So your boyfriend's in? He'll do it?"

"He said yes, he can make it happen. Twenty thousand dollars." She crossed her arms over her shirt, covering the nametag still pinned to her shirt. "By the way, sorry about all that at the Reef. I was afraid someone would see us talking and I just figure it's better if they don't."

"That's smart. I'm glad you're thinking ahead."

She seemed to glow from the praise. Dominic felt a surge of pride himself. It had been a long time since he'd had this kind of effect on anyone, especially a girl.

"So how long until I get my money?" he said.

"Six weeks."

"Why so long?"

She shrugged. "That's the normal timetable. Andy doesn't want to do anything that'll seem unusual. He's gonna put the paperwork in tomorrow, says there's some forms you need to sign first. After that it should be smooth sailing."

"Thanks for helping me out here, I appreciate it." Dominic took out his pack of smokes, lit a couple, handed one to Kat. "Tell me something—if you were me, what would you do with it, the money?"

She stared out at the ocean, took a drag, the tip of her cigarette a bright red dot in the dark. "I don't know, go to a beach, one that's far away from here. Where the air's warmer and the water's bluer. Maybe Puerto Rico or something. Not that I've ever been but it's supposed to be real nice. My dad always talked about it when I was a kid, he and my mom went there on their honeymoon."

Dominic remembered now that Kat had been raised by a single father. He had a dry cleaner's on 116th Street and whenever he showed up at school plays and stuff, he was stumbling drunk. All the other kids used to laugh at him, Dominic too.

"How's he doing these days?"

"Had a heart attack, passed about nine months ago. My mom died when I was six, so it's just me now."

"Sorry to hear that." Dominic took a drag of his cigarette, wishing he had a beer. "My dad died when I was ten. I guess I know how it feels. Losing a parent like that."

She nodded, the sound of the crashing surf filling the silence. He hadn't expected the conversation to get this heavy.

"I really should get home," Kat said, getting to her feet and stubbing out her cigarette in the sand. Dominic did the same thing.

"So soon?"

"I've got an early class in the morning."

"That's too bad. I was having fun." He was surprised to realize he meant it.

"Maybe we could do this again sometime. Here, let me give you my number. Just text me and I'll have yours too."

He handed her his phone and studied her closely. He remembered how she'd been such a target in high school, always just waiting to get hit—by a stray volleyball in gym, by a groping fist in the hallway, by a pop quiz or a dirty joke she didn't understand. Back then, he'd always thought she deserved what she got, but now he felt different. As she gave the phone back, he held onto her hand, looking into her eyes. "What would you do if I kissed you right now?" he asked.

"My boyfriend … if he knew we were out here like this …"

"So what? You think I'm scared of him?"

He felt possessive, like she was trying to take something away from him. Something else, when he'd lost so much already. But then he saw this wasn't about him. There was fear in her eyes, dark as the sky at the place where it met the water line.

"Your boyfriend, he's not a problem, Kat. We haven't done nothing anyway."

"And what if we do? What happens then?" She looked right at him, her eyes as bright as the tip of her cigarette had been. "I gotta go. He's waiting for me."

She started to walk away and Dominic grabbed her arm, pulled her close. He brought his lips to hers, gave her the kind of long deep kiss that wasn't meant to lead to anything, not yet. It was just a promise of what lay ahead. Then she pulled away again and he let her. She moved quickly toward the boardwalk, her black skirt swishing back as she moved unsteadily across the sand.

The next afternoon, Kat texted Dominic to say that everything was a go, her boyfriend had given her the paperwork for him to sign. He was eager to get this handled and—to his surprise—almost as eager to see Kat again. He told her that he could come by her place if she wanted. She texted back and said she was about to head into work but she would meet him out at the old pier at ten o'clock again, after her shift. There was a little pause and then she added: BRING A BLANKET with a smile emoji. Dominic was excited. This boyfriend of hers, they'd handle him. Soon as Dominic got his money, of course. He just had to make sure that whatever happened between then and now stayed under wraps.

Usually Dominic got right up and had breakfast, but this morning he went to the computer—his mom's ancient desktop, his laptop had gotten ruined in the flood—and started looking at one of those travel websites. He typed in Puerto Rico and saw that he could get a pretty cheap flight for two just after Thanksgiving. He looked at some pictures and was amazed at how pretty it was: impossibly blue skies, water clear as glass, caramel-colored sand. Nothing like the beach here at all.

Then again, was he really going to take Kat Griffin to Puerto Rico? There were other girls he could ask, at least a couple, who he felt sure would say yes and show him a good time. But they'd have their own ideas about what to do, and they'd surely bitch about this or that. That was the thing about Kat. She wasn't used to having a lot, so she seemed pretty happy with whatever she got.

Still, he was getting ahead of himself here, spending a chunk of his money when he didn't even have enough cash to last the next six weeks. But he had an idea about that.

A pretty good one, actually.

After breakfast, he went out and took another walk on the beach, hoping he might run into Kat on her way to work again. He didn't. He spent the rest of the day at Mulligan's, drinking and playing pool, and then he went home for dinner. Ma made eggplant parmesan, her best meal, her way of apologizing for the night before. Over dinner she reminded him that she was going out to bingo at the VFW. Forgot all about it, he said, although of course he hadn't.

He gave her twenty minutes after she left just in case she got one of her headaches and came home early, then headed for Ma's bedroom. The ring was tucked into a nest of junk jewelry, the perfect camouflage. He turned it over in his hand. A bright blue stone surrounded by silver. The insurance agent who'd come after the storm had appraised a bunch of stuff, including this, and said it was worth two thousand dollars.

A lot more than his father must've paid when they got engaged.

Not that his mother had much sentiment about the ring. She was always going on about how his father worked too much and never appreciated her, and she hadn't worn the sapphire in years. Besides, he wasn't going to get rid of it forever, just long enough to get the money he needed.

Twenty minutes later he was at the Seashell Pawn Shop, where a tattooed guy with thinning hair offered him six hundred dollars for the ring. Dominic started to haggle, but he could see he wasn't going to get anywhere with this inked-up dude. He felt a pang of regret as the clerk scooped up the ring. But it wasn't like he'd done anything permanent. As soon as the check came in, he'd get the ring back.

Easy as could be.

After that he had a little time to kill before meeting Kat, so he went home and hid the money inside a hole he'd punched in his bedroom wall. It was covered with a Metallica poster he had from high school so Ma would never think to look in there to find it. He got himself cleaned up and ready to go. Then he went into the hall closet and got that blanket Kat had asked for, along with a small cooler. He filled it with beer and headed out.

The boardwalk was quiet this time of night, except for a guy with a metal detector, another wheeling a shopping cart full of trash bags. He heard the faint titter of distant teenagers but didn't see anyone and then it got quiet again.

When he saw the gray line of the old pier in the distance, he took the steps down to the sand. His sneakers crunched as he headed toward the water, where white foam gobbled up dark sand. The breeze off the ocean was just the right hint of cool and tangy. This kind of weather probably made people think these nights would last forever, but Dominic knew better. He'd lost too much to think that anything was permanent, especially when nature was involved.

He spread the blanket on the sand and sat and waited. He opened the cooler and took out one of the beers and popped the tab. The cool liquid felt good in his mouth, and he was just swallowing it when he heard footsteps behind him.

"Hey, sorry to keep you waiting."

Kat was there, wearing her short black skirt and her low-cut T-shirt, her nametag still on. Her smile made her look as pretty as any of the girls he'd chased in high school, a few of whom he'd even caught. Right then he wouldn't have traded Kat for any of them.

"I've got the paperwork in here." She slid off a small backpack and set it down. "You want to deal with this now?"

"Let's get it out of the way," he said. "Then we can celebrate."

"Okay." She smiled shyly, rummaging in her backpack, and produced a clipboard with a wad of papers. "I'll trade you for that beer."

"Sounds like a deal."

He took the clipboard and used his phone to light the pages, signing wherever he saw an X. He glanced at Kat, who strolled toward the churning water. Her T-shirt strained a little as she tilted her head back to sip his beer, and he had to force himself to look down and focus. When he was done, he walked to the edge of the surf to join her.

She held out the can. "Take it. Otherwise, I'll finish the whole thing, and beer goes right to my head."

"I wouldn't mind seeing you a little drunk."

"I bet. Only I have a feeling I'll want to remember tonight."

He did, too. He took a long sip of the beer and stood there, feeling the faint mist on his skin.

"Did you know I had a crush on you in high school?" she asked.

"Nope." He chugged the rest of the beer. "I'm glad you told me, though."

"Wouldn't have mattered then. Fat Kat Griffin."

He crumpled the beer can, tossed it aside. "Don't say that. That's not how I see you."

"How do you see me?"

He started to answer but before he did, she was moving in for a kiss. As her lips touched his, every nerve ending in his whole body came alive. He tried to remember the last time he'd felt this good. Not since the storm, that was for sure. Maybe not since senior year of high school even. He missed that feeling of being in charge, with everyone either looking up to him or fearing him.

He pulled Kat down into the sand, moved in on top of her, kissed her some more. He started to glide his hands across her body when he began to feel the strange sensation that his fingers were somehow not attached. That was weird. He sat up then, lightheaded and queasy, the sound of the ocean both very close and impossibly far away at the same time.

"You okay, Dominic?"

Truth was, beneath his buzz of excitement he was a little woozy. He reached for the beer, then remembered he'd already finished it.

"I'm okay … just a little weird, I guess."

"Do you remember the first time we hung out here?"

"Yeah, hard to forget. Seeing as it was only last night."

"No. It wasn't."

He started to tell her he had no idea what she was talking about and then he felt a little tickle in his brain. Not a memory, more like the shadow of one.

"Back in high school, I ran into you out here one night. You'd been drinking with your friends, I guess, but they'd all gone home by then. I was out for a late-night walk. I did that sometimes, just to get away from my dad."

He listened to the sound of her voice, and heard something he didn't recognize. A hardness he'd never known was there.

"You called out to me and we sat and had a couple beers and talked. It's true, you know, I'd always had a crush on you and I was so happy to be there, and then you started kissing me. You remember that, Dominic?"

He didn't. There were some nights in high school that had gotten away from him, he knew that. Not many, but a few.

"I'd never had a real boyfriend and I told you to take it slow but you didn't, you wouldn't. I had to fight you pretty hard before you got off of me."

He looked at her with a kind of disbelief. How could this be true? He wasn't that kind of a person, and he didn't remember this at all.

"I tried to talk to you about it at school the next day, but you just ignored me, the way you always had. Before, I'd been okay with that but now it made me feel so shitty, like I was nothing. Some girl who didn't even exist."

"I didn't ... I don't remember what you're saying. If I did that ... I'm sorry, I really am."

"Shut up."

He tried to stand but his legs were wobbly. He took a step away from Kat but his foot slipped in the sand and he fell.

"What bullshit," he said, his tongue feeling fat inside his mouth. "You just ... you played me."

"Well, yes and no. Truth is, I wanted to leave this shithole years ago. The only reason I stuck around was to take care of my dad. When he finally died, I was ready to go but I needed some cash. Besides, I met this guy by then, Andy. He's really sweet. He does work for Rebuild Rockaway, you know, and we *have* run the scam I told you about, and that's given us a pretty good haul. Enough to go someplace where no one thinks of me as goddamn Fat Kat Griffin."

Dominic tried to roll over but when he put his hands down, he couldn't seem to straighten his arms. Then he looked up and saw a familiar face. Pale, blond hair drooping down. It took him a moment but then he remembered. Tim the inspector.

He must've said it aloud.

"His full name is Timothy Anderson, Junior, actually." Kat smiled. "Most people call him Tim, except close family and friends. They actually call him Andy so as not to confuse him with his dad."

"Nice to see you again, Dominic." Tim pushed a swath of blond hair out of his face. "Wish it didn't have to be like this, of course, but ..."

Tim—or Andy as Kat called him—moved in closer, and he felt something soft, the blanket, as they rolled him onto it. Then a lurch in his stomach as they lifted him into the air. They were on the move, Andy and Kat at either end of the blanket, carrying him. But where?

*Oh shit.*

"Andy's the one who started all this, you know. One day he tells me he got an application from this guy who wanted to get paid back for all this crazy shit he lost in the storm, and I asked him who it was. It was you, Dominic. And I remembered what you did and I thought, well, maybe it's time for a little payback. I gave it a couple days after you found out you weren't getting the money you wanted from Rebuild Rockaway, then followed you from home down to the boardwalk. I remembered what kind of guy you were and figured if I gave you a chance, I wouldn't even have to suggest scamming the program. You'd come up with the idea all by yourself."

He felt seasick, his body lurching as they carried him toward the water.

"Can't ... won't ... get away with ..."

"Come on, think about it. You're just some loser living in his mother's house, and everything you had washed away. Your last hope was applying for the Rebuild Rockaway program and when you got rejected, you were devastated. So you drank too much and started climbing around on the old pier and couldn't make your way back. Maybe you even wanted things to end this way. A sad story but one that won't be too hard for anyone to swallow. Not even your *Ma*."

He felt his body rolling off the blanket, the cold water lapping against his cheeks, the salt stinging his eyes. He heard whimpering sounds and realized they came from his own mouth, like he was a kitten whose tail someone had stepped on.

"Don't ... pl-pl-pl ..."

Dominic tried to say more but saltwater surged into his mouth. He struggled to twist away from the surf, but his muscles had stopped listening, and he felt himself being turned onto his back. He gagged for air, the pressure on his lungs heavy and suffocating. He thought about Puerto Rico, the so-bright blue sky overhead, the warm gentle breeze tingling his cheeks. He and Kat, they'd have a good time there, he thought, as a wall of seawater broke over his face.

# THE CORPSE AT THE FOOT OF MY BED

## Gordon Linzner

Waking up early for no reason is annoying enough. I didn't need a stranger staring at me as well.

His face pressed against the sidelight window next to my balcony door, leering up from the foot of my bed. His features were distorted, but I managed to make out clear blue eyes and dirty blond hair.

I grimaced. You'd expect more privacy in the top rear apartment of a four-story walk-up.

I glared at him.

He didn't even blink.

I thought he might go away if I went back to sleep. Better yet, I hoped I *was* still asleep, dreaming him. I shut my eyes and rolled over.

My alarm clock disagreed.

I turned back to the window. "Still there?" I muttered, adding a few choice curses. Grateful that, for a change, I'd bothered slipping on pajama bottoms the night before, I finally climbed out of bed.

I grasped a heavy bookend in my right hand and reached for the door latch with my left. My fingers paused against the cool metal. The intruder still didn't move. Now I saw why. His lips were pressed, distorted, against the glass, but the pane remained unfogged.

That wasn't fair. He wasn't *my* corpse. I hadn't put him there. And now he was my responsibility.

I backed off, took a caramel candy from the jar on my dresser and popped it in my mouth. Saliva helps me think, gets my creative juices flowing. I needed to review my options.

My balcony sat on the roof of a setback. Lower apartments in the line were roomier, compensating for the lack of an outdoor facility. Buildings on the block were attached, as were the setbacks. A shoulder-high picket fence protected me from the monotonously non-flowering illicit plants cultivated by my neighbor to the west. Even were that vegetation thick enough to conceal a body for a day or two, said neighbor would almost certainly toss it back on my side.

That might even be how the body got here in the first place.

I considered heaving the corpse over my waist-high railing. It would land in the backyard of the ground floor tenant, a nice white-haired lady who'd tried to look after my cat while I was in hospital. That seemed ungrateful. It wasn't her fault the animal got out of the backyard, onto the street, to get hit by a cab. I still sometimes need to remind myself not to blame her.

Both plans were deeply flawed. Forty or fifty rear apartments on the next block faced mine. So did the upper floors of the hotel across from them. There was certain to be someone watching.

This was a two caramel problem.

How much did the dead man weigh? More than my slender frame could handle, I guessed. With a baggage carrier, I might wrestle him downstairs and over two blocks to the Hudson River, but there was the same issue of observers. If there's anything residents of Manhattan's Upper West Side enjoy more than spying on neighbors from their windows, it's doing so from their stoops. Even at six in the morning.

I contemplated other increasingly grisly and ridiculous scenarios for disposal. Once they were out of my system, I did what I knew I would have to do all along.

I phoned the police.

I heated enough hot water for a dozen cups of tea or instant coffee, as a courtesy to my official visitors. The fresh mug of cocoa was for me. My sour stomach deserved some pampering.

Lieutenant Chesney, the lead detective, arrived with his team within half an hour of the uniformed police. His shoulders were broad. He smelled of peanuts. His sky-blue tie was knotted left of center. He didn't want a caramel. His questions mostly mirrored those the officers had already asked. I pretended they were new. Neither of us was fooled.

"The name Roger Baker means nothing to you?" They'd gotten that, presumably with other details, from his wallet.

"I'd never seen the man before. Under any name."

Chesney scribbled in his notebook. "That's an interesting qualification."

"His ID might be phony." I finished my cocoa, frowning at the scum of chocolate that always remains on the bottom, no matter how much I stir. "My apologies. It's a mental trick I use to calm myself. I look at what's bothering me from every angle. The less likely the scenario, the better. It gives my mind something to do, helps soothe my nerves."

"You're nervous now?"

"Shouldn't I be?"

"You don't act it. You seem to be taking this whole thing in stride."

I set down my empty cup and met the detective's pale green eyes. "Two years ago, I had a psychotic episode that put me in the hospital for a month. I'm mostly fine now, so long as I keep up my medication and avoid unnecessary mental stress. I don't enjoy having a dozen officers and detectives cluttering up my bedroom and balcony—who would?—but I can't afford to let it bother me."

Chesney scribbled some more. "Which hospital?"

I told him, adding the names of my doctors and the pharmacy that filled my prescription every month. I even offered to show him my pills. He shook his head.

"Later. Maybe. How do you think Roger Baker got onto your balcony, Mr. Conway?"

"I assume he fell from the roof."

"That would make quite a thud. Didn't it wake you?"

You shouldn't smile when a cop is asking questions. I couldn't help it. "I sleep through all kinds of noise in this neighborhood, Lieutenant. Cats in heat. Blaring stereos. Would-be singers."

"At three in the morning?"

"Frequently. Is that when Baker landed?"

"You tell me."

"I don't know. I went to bed around ten. Read for a while before falling asleep. He was there when I woke, just before six. Maybe the new tenant in the downstairs apartment heard something."

"We'll get to her." Chesney gnawed the top of his ballpoint pen, clicking the push-button with his tongue, flipping through his notebook. Then he put it aside. "I buy your story about avoiding stress, Mr. Conway, so I'm going to tell you something I shouldn't. I can't give you a clean bill of health until our investigation is complete, but

I personally don't see you as a murderer."

I wiped wet palms on my slacks. "Murder? I thought maybe he had a heart attack. I didn't see any blood. The drop from the roof isn't enough to kill a person, unless you land just right. Or wrong, rather."

Chesney cleared his throat. "We still have to go over your entire apartment, make absolutely certain he was never a visitor, invited or not. This is all of it? Bedroom, living room, bathroom, kitchenette?"

"If you find another room, don't tell the owner. He'll raise my rent."

Chesney shut his eyes and sighed. "Our forensic team will be here for a while," he added. "In the meantime, I'd like you to come down to the station and make a formal statement."

I agreed with a shrug. I could use the fresh air.

I called my office from Chesney's desk. The supervisor didn't appreciate my taking off a day so near the end of a fiscal quarter, but she said nothing. Better I miss a day now than spend another stressed-out month in hospital. By doing my duty as a citizen, I also received part of my city taxes back in the form of a ham on rye and a lukewarm Coke.

A few police were still wandering my building's roof when I returned to my apartment, looking for signs of a struggle and, I gathered, finding none. I was ordered to avoid the balcony for the next few days, in case they'd missed something they didn't yet know they were looking for. No problem. I hadn't much chance to enjoy the space since the gardener started sampling his crop nightly.

Sipping fresh cocoa, I focused on the sidelight window through which Baker's corpse stared at me a few hours earlier. White police tape marked the body's outline. Something else was different; it took me a moment to see it.

Through the narrow gaps between slats of the picket fence, the planters next door were barren. For a while, at least, the evening air would be fresh.

Then my horticultural neighbor came into view. He was shirtless; for all I knew, his only garment might've been his yellow headband. He glared sulkily at his ruined agriculture, then spotted me smiling from my bedroom. I must have looked insufferably smug.

"You son of a bitch!" His voice carried easily through the glass. "Why didn't you warn me those pigs were coming?"

Obviously, he'd also been visited that morning. I opened a vent beside the door to reply. "You didn't ask."

"Do you know what you cost me? How much Mary Jane I had to flush down the toilet? Which is clogged now, so thanks for that, too."

I toyed with the unlikely idea the dead man might have been a customer of his. Maybe a supplier. Or a rival. "I'm not particularly interested," I answered, "but feel free to tell the rest of our neighbors."

He looked around, blinking, as if for the first time realizing, or caring, how well voices carried in the artificial canyon between row buildings. He stormed back inside. A moment later, his stereo began throbbing on the other side of my bedroom wall.

I carried my jar of caramels into the living room and turned on my television in self defense. John Wayne had just discovered Natalie Wood living with the Comanches. My neighbor wasn't smart enough to make the slightest attempt at concealing his plants, let alone commit murder.

I followed an early dinner with a long hot bath, made fresh cocoa, and settled down with a vintage Wodehouse novel. Rolls were just starting to fly at the Drones Club when my door buzzer blatted. I groaned, put down the book, tightened my robe's belt, and moved to the intercom next to the door.

Silently, I leaned one ear against the speaker. No sound came from the vestibule. Some of the kids on the block liked to play these games.

As I moved away the buzzer sounded again.

"Who's there?" I snapped.

"Sandra Martin. From 3B."

Her voice was slightly muffled by the coat I kept hanging on my door. Why didn't she just knock?

The fish-eye peephole lens thickened her nose, making the rest of her features look more pinched than I remembered from the few times we passed in the hall. Her yellow beehive hairdo was adequate identification though.

I opened the door.

"We haven't been introduced," I greeted. "I'm Fred Conway."

In her late twenties, I guessed, Sandra already showed faint wrinkles at the corners of her cool gray eyes and narrow smile. Her skin spent too much time in the sun, retaining its deep tan. Off-white lipstick was the only noticeable sign of makeup. Her jeans were so snug I could have counted the change in her pocket; her t-shirt was not designed to keep my blood pressure steady.

"Hi, Fred. I moved in last month."

"I know. What can I do for you, Sandra?"

She licked her lips. I wondered if the lipstick was flavored. "I spoke to the police today. They said you found a body on your balcony."

"I'd guess they spoke to lots of people about that."

She flashed straight, white, perfectly aligned teeth. "May I come in?"

I fingered my bathrobe's lapel. "I'm not exactly dressed for company."

"I won't stay long. It's just, well, exciting. I've never been part of anything like this before. I want to hear all about it." Her gray eyes glistened.

I let her in, mostly to spare other tenants the echo of our voices in the hall. "I don't know much," I warned.

"Well, I don't know anything."

Sandra turned down my offer of cocoa. She toyed with a piece of caramel without unwrapping it. We sat staring at each other for a long moment, undoubtedly more pleasurable for me than her.

Finally, she said, "I'm being insensitive. It must have been awful for you."

"I've had happier experiences."

"Do the police have any leads? Any clue what might have happened?"

"They didn't confide in me."

"They asked if I knew a Roger Baker. Was that his name?"

"Probably. A person is more than a name."

She leaned forward, again sampling her upper lip with her tongue. I admired her shirt's tensile strength as she scratched her shoulder. "I'm surprised they didn't take you in. As a suspect."

I ticked off reasons on my fingers. "No motive. No means. No proof Baker was ever in my apartment. They had no choice but to look elsewhere. That's why we pay taxes."

Her frown was more natural than her smile. "You don't want me here, do you?"

My terry-cloth robe soaked up most of my perspiration. I sipped my cocoa and placed the cup on the lamp table, next to Wodehouse.

"My apologies, Sandra. It's been an unnerving day. I need to go to work tomorrow. Let me make up for my boorishness over dinner. Is Friday good? By then I may have a few more gory details to share."

Her left hand, presumably trying to lean atop the lamp table, brushed my cup. Her right more easily located my cheek. Her fingers smelled of strawberry.

"I'd like that," she said.

I heard her heels clatter down the stairs. Her door creaked open. Locks fell into place behind her.

Something else fell into place for me.

Sandra may have visited me out of morbid curiosity, or actual concern, or any number of reasons. One stood out.

I stared at my half-full cup of cocoa, untouched since her visit. In the short run, it would be easy to pour the stuff down the drain, wash out the cup, pretend the whole thing never happened. In the long run, I didn't dare forget it.

Sandra would try again.

I covered the cup with cling-wrap and placed it in the fridge. It took a minute to locate the precinct's phone number, another to reach their Homicide division.

I asked for Lieutenant Chesney.

"He's off duty. Can I help?"

I dried my free hand on my robe. "I don't know. Are you working the Roger Baker murder?"

"I'm familiar with it."

"What kind of poison did the autopsy find?"

"I'm not at liberty to reveal those details. Who did you say you were?"

"I didn't say. Fred Conway. I found the body." My claim to fame.

"You have further information?"

You don't hedge with the police. Either tell the truth or lie outright. "Just curious. Tell the lieutenant I called."

"You bet I will."

"I'll be home the rest of the evening."

I rang off and waited for Chesney to get back to me. I knew he would. He'd never mentioned poison.

The stuff must not have been a hundred percent effective. Baker somehow managed to climb out a rear window and up the rough brick wall one flight to my balcony, only to die at my door. The exertion likely hastened his reaction. I didn't know, or care, why Sandra Martin killed him.

Her attempt on a stranger's life, mine, made sense. If I were found dead of the same poison, it might be chalked up to a remorseful suicide; Chesney would drop the investigation, along with any line of inquiry leading to my downstairs neighbor.

*Might* wasn't good enough; she'd want additional insurance.

I found that insurance under the cushion of her chair, along with her still unwrapped caramel. I didn't touch the silver cufflink, unwilling to disturb any fingerprints, but I could see it bore the letter B in an Old English font.

His name really might be Baker, then.

I reached for the Wodehouse, changed my mind. I knew I wouldn't be able to concentrate.

My boss was really going to hate my being out two days in a row, so close to the fiscal quarter's end. 🔫

# POISONED RELATIONSHIP

## A You-Solve-It By Laird Long

One lady brought a recipe for death ...

"You're the first to arrive!" Mabel greeted Grace, bustling her friend into her living room. "The tea's just brewing now. Make yourself comfortable."

Grace walked around the glass-topped coffee table and sat down on the quilt-covered couch against the wall. As Mabel turned her back on her guest and hustled over to the front window, looking out for her other three expected guests.

Every Thursday afternoon, the five old friends—Mabel, Grace, Iris, Daphne, and Enid—got together for tea and dainties; to chat, exchange recipes, show off their latest handicrafts, and discuss TV shows they'd watched. This particular Thursday, it was Mabel's turn to host.

"Here they are now!" the woman exclaimed. She rushed to the front door and flung it open. "Come in, come in! The tea's just about ready."

Mabel prided herself on her teawomanship, and the special recipe she used to bake her famous cookies.

Iris, Daphne, and Enid trooped through the front door and into the living room. Iris and Daphne joined Grace on the couch, while Enid sat down in one of the two chairs that flanked the large coffee table at either end.

"I think the tea is ready!" Mabel announced. She hurried out of the living room and turned down the short hall to the kitchen in back.

Grace followed after her. "I'll help you with the tea, Mabel!"

The two women were soon back, Mabel carrying a tray bearing her silver tea set, Grace holding another tray on which five china teacups were arranged. They carefully set the trays down on the coffee table.

Mabel then poured, passed the cups of tea around to her guests. Finally, she sat down in the other chair, with her cup of tea.

"Delicious," the women complimented their beaming host, as they sipped their tea.

Then the five got down to the serious business of neighbourhood gossip.

"Oh! The cookies!" Mabel suddenly interjected, interrupting her own story about her new next-door neighbour. "I almost forgot!"

"You finish your story," Enid said, rising to her feet. "I'll get the cookies."

"They're in the cupboard over the sink!" Mabel yelled after the woman.

There was a loud bang outside, and Mabel twisted her head around and glanced out the front window. "Oh! There's my new neighbour now!"

She got to her feet and rushed over to the window, waving at the others. "See how handsome he is, ladies!"

Iris and Grace set their cups down on the coffee table and got off the couch. They went over to the window to admire the view of Mabel's neighbour out on his front lawn next-door.

Daphne remained on the couch. "You girls are incorrigible," she admonished good-naturedly.

A few moments later, Enid returned to the living room with a plateful of cookies. "What's all the excitement?" she asked, setting the plate down on the coffee table.

"Oh, he's gone inside now. Show's over, ladies," Mabel laughed, turning back to Daphne and Enid.

The women resumed their seats, and all five sipped their tea and sampled the cookies.

Until Iris set her teacup down and swallowed a last piece of cookie and said, "I have to use the little girls' room." She left the living room, headed down the hallway opposite for the bathroom at the end.

Only a few seconds after that, Mabel suddenly coughed, spluttered. The half-eaten cookie dropped out of her left hand, the half-empty cup of tea out of her right. She clutched her throat, sitting bolt upright. Then she collapsed down onto the floor.

"Poisoned," one of the paramedics pronounced, kneeling next to Mabel's body on the carpet.

The pair of emergency responders had rolled up to Mabel's house four minutes after the frantic call had come in.

Grace, Iris, Daphne, and Enid all gasped, their hands jumping up to their own throats, their eyes jumping down to the tea service and plate of cookies on the coffee table.

"I don't think any of you will be affected, if you haven't been already," the second paramedic tried to reassure the women standing together in the living room. "The poison was obviously fast-acting, and targeted."

Who poisoned Mabel?

Solution in next month's issue ...

# SOLUTION TO JUNE'S YOU-SOLVE-IT

## GALLERY THIEF BY PETER DICHELLIS

"I figured the Farthington couple set up the theft to collect the insurance money," Dalpaz continued. "But I was wrong. Why'd you zero-in on Lew Temkins? His alibi seemed solid to me."

Detective Muldoon smiled. "I only asked Temkins for an alibi, nothing more specific. His answer revealed he was aware the crime occurred between 9 pm and 10 pm last night, something only the thief would know."

"Sounds like he painted himself into a corner," Dalpaz said.

Manufactured by Amazon.ca
Bolton, ON

45790071R00046